A PEEK INSIDE

Ethan slid off the wagon seat and dropped to the ground. Clutching the flour sack, he surveyed his new home while the stationmaster lifted his sister and his little brothers from the wagon. Fields stretched as far as he could see around the building, but large trees shaded the yard. It seemed a long way to walk from the road to the broad steps that led to the front door of the Home.

The sun was sinking behind the roof, and Ethan's heart sank with it. But he mustn't let the others know. They depended on him. So once again he straightened his shoulders and tried to look in charge.

"Take Simon's hand, Alice," he told his sister, "and I'll hold Will." To the stationmaster he added, "Thank you, sir. We'll be fine now."

BEYOND THE ORPHAN TRAIN SERIES

Looking for Home

Whistle-Stop West

Prairie Homestead

Across the Border

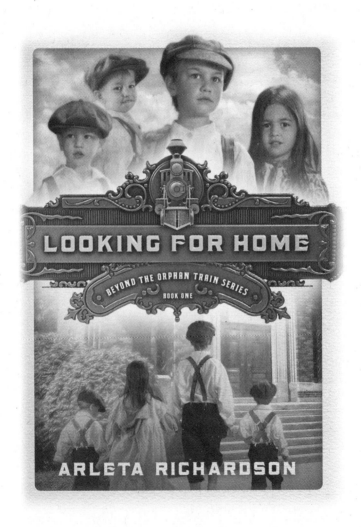

LOOKING FOR HOME

BEYOND THE ORPHAN TRAIN SERIES

BOOK ONE

ARLETA RICHARDSON

DAVID C COOK

transforming lives together

LOOKING FOR HOME
Published by David C Cook
4050 Lee Vance Drive
Colorado Springs, CO 80918 U.S.A.

Integrity Music Limited, a Division of David C Cook
Brighton, East Sussex BN1 2RE, England

The graphic circle C logo is a registered trademark of David C Cook.

This story is a work of fiction. All characters and events are
the product of the author's imagination. Any resemblance
to any person, living or dead, is coincidental.

All Scripture quotations are taken from the King James
Version of the Bible. (Public Domain.)

Library of Congress Control Number 2015952817
ISBN 978-1-4347-0955-4
eISBN 978-1-4347-0229-6

The Team: Catherine DeVries, Ramona Tucker, Ingrid Beck, Amy
Konyndyk, Jon Middel, Nick Lee, Tiffany Thomas, Susan Murdock
Cover Design: DogEared Design, Kirk DouPonce
Cover Photo: Kirk DouPonce and iStockphoto

Printed in the United States of America
Second Edition 2016

8 9 10 11 12 13 14 15 16 17

120820

To John and Jennie
With God's help they made a success
of all that life handed them.

CONTENTS

Chapter One

ETHAN TAKES CHARGE

Outside Jefferson, Pennsylvania
May 1907

Beads of sweat stood on Ethan Cooper's upper lip. It wasn't long past sunup and was sure hot for May. Keeping a careful hand on the squirming baby, he reached for the flannel that had been his ma's petticoat. It was an awful lot of cloth, but nothing else was suitable for a diaper. He fastened the bottom of the petticoat with two big pins and then wrapped the rest around the baby several times to cover her.

"Doesn't look right to me," said five-year-old Alice, who knelt on the floor nearby.

He glanced down. "You should talk. How will you fasten your stockings to your vest? You put it on backwards."

"Had to. Can't reach the buttons if they're in the back."

"Stand up and turn around. I'll fasten it for you. Then I've got to dress the boys. Mrs. Kenny'll be here soon."

"Are we really going to leave Molly with her?" Alice asked, her brown eyes troubled as she got to her feet. Her gaze lingered on his face for a moment before she turned around.

"We don't have a choice, Allie," he said as he helped her with the vest. "The Home won't take little babies. You heard Russell say that he almost couldn't get Will in."

Ethan was glad that Alice had her back to him now. An eight-year-old boy couldn't let his sister see the tears that came no matter how hard he swallowed.

"Now, put your dress on and brush your hair," he told her in a kind voice. "I'll braid it when I finish here."

As he helped dress Simon and Will, his two little brothers, Ethan reflected on the days that had led up to this morning. Until a few months ago, his life had been pretty ordinary. The Cooper clan—Ma, Pa, and their nine children, with Ethan smack in the middle—had never known anything but the drafty, run-down house on the desolate edge of nowhere, a long walk from the town of Jefferson. Didn't everyone have burlap stretched over broken windows and cracks a boy could stick his hand through? But it was home, and they were content.

Ethan was old enough to know they wouldn't have fared even as well as they had, if it weren't for Mary and Seth Kenny. Since Pa was away from home more than he was there, the family would have been hungry and cold many times had it not been for their kind neighbors. Before Molly was born, Ma used to rock Will in the evening and tell the children about the year she and Pa moved to this house.

"That was before any of you were born," Ma had said. "The Kennys helped us move in." She looked around the room and sighed. "It looked worse than this back then. But we were glad to have a home. Still, seems like Pa never got around to fixing things up much."

"Where's Pa?" Simon's voice broke into Ethan's thoughts.

"I told you. He's gone to work on a boat."

"Is he coming back?"

"Probably not," Ethan replied. "But it doesn't matter. We won't be here."

Simon nodded and submitted to the wet comb going through his hair. Ethan knew the little boy wouldn't ask about Ma. Simon hadn't mentioned her since the day he sat under the kitchen table and watched the men carry her out to the cemetery. No one had even thought to look for Simon until late that evening when Rachel, their older sister, had discovered him, asleep under the table, and put him to bed.

"He won't remember," she had said. "He's too young."

It seemed that she was right. Simon had awakened the next morning and joined the others at the table as usual. He didn't even look toward the bed where Ma had been lying for so many weeks.

It must be easier to forget when you're only three, Ethan thought. Just last month, Simon had turned four … without Ma there to celebrate with them.

Ethan hadn't forgotten. He didn't say anything about missing Ma, mostly because no one talked about it. But once in a while, the subject came up.

"Why did Jesus take Ma to heaven, Ethan?" Alice asked once.

"Ma was tired, Allie. It's hard to get any rest when there are nine kids in the house. Remember she read to us from the Bible where Jesus said, 'Come unto me, all ye that labour and are heavy laden, and I will give you rest'? So that's what He did. He gave her rest."

One part of Ethan was glad Ma wasn't sick any longer. But a bigger part wished she would come back. He needed help taking care of things.

He didn't need it bad enough to wish that Pa would come home, though. Ethan glanced at the lard pail that served as Pa's lunch bucket. How many times had he been ordered to trudge into town to get that bucket filled with beer for Pa? More times than Ethan wanted to remember. In fact, there wasn't much about Pa that Ethan did want to remember. How disappointed he'd been when Pa refused to allow him to go to Sunday school with the Kennys.

"I don't want the church folks thinking they have to give their old clothes to my family," Pa had declared. "We'll get along on our own."

Well, that was past. Ethan wouldn't be going after Pa's beer again. And he had known for some time that his three older brothers and sister wouldn't be able to support the family for long. He had heard Russell and the others discussing it.

"What can we do, Russ?" Rachel had asked. "Someone has to look after them better than we've been doing. Ethan shouldn't have to take care of Molly. Simon and Will are more than enough for him to watch. He won't get to school at all this fall if we leave it like this."

Russell had nodded and slumped in his chair. "I know. With you working out at the Higgins place, and Walter, Jake, and me finding jobs where we can …" Suddenly Russell looked almost as old as Pa. Then he leaned forward. "I've been thinking on it. I heard about this county asylum over at Briarlane. Mr. Peat's hired man used to live there. They take orphans until they're sixteen. We could send the little ones. Even if Pa is still living, we're not going to get any help from him."

"You going to send all of 'em?" Walter asked.

"Not the baby. They won't take infants. Just Alice, Simon, Will, and Ethan. Mrs. Kenny says she'll keep Molly."

"I'm big," Ethan had protested. "I can look after myself when you're gone. And I'll go to school every day. Do I have to leave?"

Rachel hugged him. "You're only eight, honey. You need someone to cook for you and take care of your clothes. Besides, the little boys need you. What would they do in a strange home with no big brother? They're too young to understand not being with family."

Ethan reluctantly agreed to leave the only home he had ever known.

Now the morning of departure had come. There wasn't much to get ready. Rachel wrote a letter and tucked it into a flour sack. Then she packed the few garments they wouldn't be wearing, and the belongings of all four children barely made a bulge in the flour sack.

Besides the clothes, each of them had a personal treasure. Alice was taking the rag doll that Ma had made for her. Simon had a whistle Jake offered him as a going-away gift. Will wouldn't part from his "pony"—a cherry-wood branch with a leather strap nailed to it. As for Ethan, his treasure was known only to himself. It was an old watch case he had found in the field. Inside he had placed a picture of Ma.

Just that instant Ethan was startled out of his memories by Will's hollering. The little boy's ear had been scrubbed enough. Quickly Ethan helped Will put on long black stockings, short pants, and cotton shirt and then plopped his brother on the bed beside the baby.

The sun was higher now. He'd have to hurry and get himself ready to leave. Mrs. Kenny would arrive any minute to walk into town with them and meet the streetcar that would take them to the county seat. From there they would be on their own.

Mrs. Kenny appeared as Ethan finished combing his hair. She was cheerful as she wrapped Molly in her shawl and grasped Alice by the hand.

"Have your trolley money, do you?" she asked.

Ethan dug into his pocket and pulled out the three nickels Russ had given him for the fare. "Rachel says it won't cost anything for Will if I hold him. He's still two. He won't be three until next month."

"Hmmph," Mrs. Kenny snorted. "They aren't losing any money. All four of you would fit on one seat. But they'll fatten you up at the Home. Hear tell they have a farm and a big garden."

Ethan had decided not to think about Briarlane any sooner than he had to, but Simon heard the word *farm*.

"Cows? Will they have cows and horses?" the just-turned-four-year-old asked.

"Wouldn't be surprised," Mrs. Kenny answered. "Probably pigs, chickens, and whatever else they run on those places. You'll have lots to eat and maybe learn to farm, too. Well, are we ready?"

The younger children followed her out the door, but Ethan stood for a moment looking around the familiar room. In spite of Rachel's assurance that they would be back home as soon as things were better, he had a feeling he wouldn't see this house again. A lump formed in his throat. He shut the door swiftly and then dashed after the others.

The walk to town would take longer than usual, because Will had to be carried part of the way. They weren't out of sight of the house when Alice stopped in the road.

"Lolly!" she cried.

Mrs. Kenny stopped too. "What's the matter? What's a lolly?"

"Her doll," Ethan answered. "Wait here. I'll run back and get it."

The little boys flopped on the ground, and Mrs. Kenny leaned against a fence post.

"We'll never make it to town at this rate," she said. "Don't know why I didn't think of it sooner. Ethan, as long as you're going back, get my boys' wagon to carry these young ones."

The going was a little faster after that. Still, it was almost two hours later when Mrs. Kenny and the children stood in front of the hotel where the streetcar would pick them up. The sky had darkened, and heavy clouds promised a shower.

If only Rachel and the boys were here to see us off, Ethan thought. But of course they had to work.

Ethan straightened his shoulders and tried to look like an older brother who could take charge. He was responsible now.

Chapter Two

THE JOURNEY TO BRIARLANE

Ethan watched the rain trickle down the streetcar window and shifted as much as he could without waking Will. In the seat across from him, Alice and Simon were sleeping. Ethan's eyes were heavy, but he dared not close them. He had promised to keep watch over the children, and if he failed, they might be put off the trolley.

The motorman hadn't been pleased when the conductor lifted the three little ones up the trolley steps. He eyed them suspiciously when Ethan held out the three nickels.

"What's this?" he said. "Where's your folks?"

"There's just us," Ethan replied. "I've got money for our fare."

The man surveyed the group. Will clutched his stick horse. Simon stood wide-eyed and silent. Alice hugged her doll tightly, keeping one hand on Ethan's jacket. For a long minute the motorman looked from one to the other of the children, stopping at Ethan, who held the flour sack and Will together under one arm.

"You in charge?" he challenged Ethan.

"Yes, sir."

"Where are you going?"

"To Briarlane."

The man scowled. "Hmm. That's the end of the line. We won't get there for a couple of hours." He scanned the silent group. "You be sure they don't run around the aisles, or I'll have to put you off. And don't you be blowing that whistle." He jabbed a thumb at Simon's treasure.

"He won't, sir," Ethan reassured the man. "We'll all be quiet and sit still."

"See that you do. And stay up here at the front where I can keep an eye on you."

The nickels were given up, and Ethan shepherded his sister and brothers to the first vacant seats that faced each other.

"Ethan, can I sit by the window?" Alice whispered, sounding anxious.

Ethan nodded. "You can take turns. When we stop, trade places with Simon. That way you can both see out."

The plan worked well. Since no one dared risk the motor-man's wrath, there was no bickering or crying. The swaying of the car, the rumble of the wheels, and the splashing of the rain soon lulled the little ones to sleep. In a very short time, Ethan's eyes closed too, and he slept as the trolley rattled through the villages and fields toward the county seat.

A hand shook Ethan's shoulder, and a voice brought him upright in his seat.

"Wake up, boy. This here's the end of the line." The motor-man stood in the aisle looking down at the children. "Someone supposed to meet you young 'uns here?"

It took a moment for Ethan's mind to clear. Then he shook his head. "No, sir. We don't know anybody in this town."

The man stared at him. "Tarnation!" he exploded. "What did you come for, then?" He stared out the window at the driving rain and then down at his watch. "I got to get back on my run, but I can't put you out on the road in this drencher. You'd all drown in five minutes." He looked at the conductor standing in the doorway and gave a helpless shrug. "Now what do we do?"

"Better take 'em into the waiting room, Del. Maybe someone will be along to pick them up. I'll take the little gal if you can grab the boys, and we'll make a run for it."

Before he had time to think it through, Ethan was following the conductor and the motorman through the downpour toward the small station. The flour sack slapped against his legs as he ran, and water splashed into his boots.

In spite of their best efforts, four bedraggled and dripping children stood in the center of a room lined with benches. Ethan peered around cautiously as the men shook the raindrops from their slickers. There seemed to be only two other people present—a man behind a window and a woman sitting on a bench.

The man at the window spoke. "Who you got there, Del? Did you fish them out of the river?" He chuckled at his own question.

Del apparently failed to see the humor of it. He glared at the stationmaster as he smacked his wet hat against the wall. "They'll be fishing you out of the river if you ain't careful," he muttered. "I picked these here kids up at Jefferson, and I don't know where they go."

The stationmaster sauntered around the counter and spoke to Ethan. "Where you going, boy?"

"To the county 'sylum. Is this it?"

"Tarnation!" exclaimed the stationmaster. "Orphans! Who sent them out alone this far? And on a day like this?"

"'Tweren't their folks, I reckon," the conductor commented. Then he turned to Ethan. "Does anyone at the Home know you're coming?"

Ethan shrugged. "I don't know. Is this the place?"

Simon suddenly found his voice. "Are the cows out in back?"

Before any of the men could answer, the woman spoke. "Those children are soaked to the hide. Isn't anyone going to dry them off before they shake to death?"

Indeed the four of them were shivering, and Will's teeth chattered.

The stationmaster led them over to the stove in the corner. "Stand here and dry off a bit," he instructed. "This isn't the Home, but I suppose someone will have to see that you get there."

The children huddled around the heat, and Ethan listened as the men debated their immediate future.

"I got to get that trolley back on the road," Del insisted. "We can't do anything about them."

"Well, I can't leave here until closing time." The station-master scratched his head. "I could show 'em the way, but they can't walk in this. Botheration! Guess they'll have to stay here until I lock up. I can drop 'em off on my way home."

Will tugged on Ethan's jacket. "Hungry."

"We'll have to wait until we get to the Home," Ethan told him. "Rachel says they have lots of good food there."

At the mention of Rachel, Alice burst into tears, and Will began to wail with her. Simon's lower lip trembled, and Ethan hurried to calm the storm.

"Hey … don't worry. We'll be there pretty soon, and you'll like it. Remember the animals and the garden? If you keep howling like that, we'll get put out in the rain. At least we're warm in here."

"Tarnation," Del muttered as he dug into his pocket. "Here, boy. You can have this nickel back. You didn't take up much space." He pulled a packet out of his slicker. "I don't need no lunch. Too late to eat it now, anyway. Feed the little kids there."

Ethan gratefully accepted the offering, and the Coopers were soon munching on big sandwiches, pickles, and cookies. The woman departed with the trolley, and the stationmaster was left to oversee his unusual customers.

Ethan had no problem keeping an eye on his sister and brothers during the long, wet afternoon. They were too awed by the strange circumstances to move around the station, and when they spoke to each other, it was in whispers. As for Ethan, his best imagination couldn't picture the home and life that lay ahead of them. He waited patiently for the station to close and the trip to Briarlane to begin.

The children watched with interest as the wagon covered the distance between the trolley station and the edge of town. Their guide, the stationmaster, pointed out the landmarks with the wagon whip.

"That there's the county seat."

Ethan stared in wonder at the three-story brick building. It didn't look like a seat to him, but this man must know.

"Here's your schoolhouse. You been to school yet?"

"Yes, sir. But Alice hasn't. She can write her name and say her letters, though," he hastened to add. "Ma taught her."

On the outskirts of Briarlane, the wagon stopped in the road that ran past another large brick building. An arched sign over the entrance proclaimed Briarlane Christian Children's Home.

"Is this the 'sylum?" Ethan asked.

"Yep."

Ethan slid off the wagon seat and dropped to the ground. Clutching the flour sack, he surveyed his new home while the stationmaster lifted his sister and his little brothers from the wagon. Fields stretched as far as he could see around the building, but large trees shaded the yard. It seemed a long way to walk from the road to the broad steps that led to the front door of the Home.

The sun was sinking behind the roof, and Ethan's heart sank with it. But he mustn't let the others know. They depended on him. So once again he straightened his shoulders and tried to look in charge.

"Take Simon's hand, Alice," he told his sister, "and I'll hold Will." To the stationmaster he added, "Thank you, sir. We'll be fine now."

Chapter Three

THE BRIARS

Most of the residents of Briarlane referred to the county children's home as "that shabby old building at the edge of town."

Shabby was evidently in the eye of the beholder, for Ethan Cooper was sure they were approaching a palace. The closer they came to the big front door, the slower Ethan walked. Could this really be the place Russell had told them about? Ethan had never seen a building so grand. Surely they wouldn't be able to live here! He grasped Will's hand tighter and pulled the little boy up the steps. Should they open the door and walk in, or did one knock at such a place?

The decision was made for him as Simon stood on tiptoe and grabbed a round handle in the center of the door. A sharp bell rang in response, and the little boy dropped the handle and ducked behind his brother. Ethan was frightened but held his ground. After all, where could they go now?

He heard the echo of the clanging bell. Then voices sounded clearly through the heavy door.

"Who has door duty this week?"

"I do. I'm going."

Running footsteps sounded, and the door was jerked open. A girl of about twelve stared with an open mouth at the group arranged before her, unattended by any adult.

"Where'd you come from?" the girl blurted. She scanned the road. "Who brought you?"

"I did," Ethan replied.

"You never! How old are you?" Blue eyes challenged Ethan.

"I'm eight years old, and I did so!" Ethan was indignant. Maybe they wouldn't let them stay, but he wasn't going to have his word doubted.

"Who is it, Shala?" a soft voice asked from the hallway.

"I don't know, Mrs. Lehman. There's four of them, and a boy says he brought them."

"Well, bring them in and close the door."

Shala stepped back, allowing the children to come into the warm hallway.

Ethan gazed around in awe. Straight ahead a wide staircase led to the upper floor. He could hear feet running and voices calling to one another. The aroma of fresh bread wafted from the back of the building. Suddenly Ethan realized that he was terribly hungry.

His heart pounded as he looked at the lady standing before them. What if there was no room for them? Or worse yet, what if this lady didn't want them? He might get along all right, but what would happen to the others? For the first time that day, Ethan felt real fear.

"You've come by yourselves?" the soft voice asked.

"Yes, ma'am. We came on the trolley, and the man from the station brought us here. Is this the 'sylum?"

"This is the children's home, yes. You are just in time for supper. Shala, take them up to Matron to get ready. We'll talk after you've eaten." She put her hand gently on Ethan's shoulder and smiled at him. "What are your names?"

"I'm Ethan. This is Alice and Simon and Will."

The woman nodded. "I'm Mrs. Lehman. Matron will take care of you. Run along now."

Shala tossed her head and marched down the hallway with her nose in the air. "You can follow me if you want to." Her stiff back proclaimed clearly that these strangers weren't her problem.

Being on door duty didn't mean she was responsible for what came through it.

When Ethan and his siblings returned to the main floor with Matron for supper, the long tables in the dining room seemed crowded with children of all ages. It was a bewildering sight. The Cooper family shrank back against the door as twenty-six pairs of eyes turned toward them.

The lady with the soft voice came to their rescue. "We have a surprise tonight, everyone. Here are four more children come to stay. Bert, will you come and take Ethan to your table? And Betsy, make room for Alice next to you. Simon and Will may sit with Matron tonight."

A freckle-faced boy grinned cheerfully and led Ethan to a seat. Alice went with Betsy, and Matron shepherded the two little boys to a table. Everyone became silent, and with her head bowed, the lady spoke again.

"Lord, thank You for this day and for the rain that has blessed the earth. You have given us this food, and we are grateful. Bless the new children who have come to be with us. We welcome them in Your name. Amen."

Large bowls of soup, thick with meat and vegetables, were ladled out. Slices of bread and butter were passed around. And wonder of wonders, every child had a mug of cold milk!

Alice glanced furtively around the table, and then Ethan heard her ask Betsy, "Can we eat all this, or must we save some for tomorrow?"

"You eat it all. You can have more if you want it. We have lots of food here. We grow our own gardens."

This was hard to believe. The garden at home had never produced a meal like this. Ethan ate gratefully, and from the look of it, his siblings did too.

By the time supper was over, Will had fallen asleep with his head on the table. Matron picked him up.

"You come with us," she said to Simon. "Betsy, take Alice up to the girls' room. Ethan, Mr. Lehman will see you in the office. Bert will take you there."

Ethan watched anxiously as his brothers and sister were led away, and then he followed Bert down the long hallway and into the office. Mrs. Lehman sat in a chair, and Mr. Lehman stood at his desk studying the letter Rachel had put in the flour sack with their clothes.

Ethan waited patiently as Mr. Lehman read aloud.

Dear Sir,

Our pa has left us, and us older ones can't take care of the little ones any longer. They are good and won't be any trouble.

Ethan Allen, born November 17, 1898
Alice Carol, born July 24, 1901
Simon Peter, born April 24, 1903
William Andrew, born June 22, 1904

Rachel Cooper

"This doesn't tell us much," George Lehman said. "We'll have to try and locate the father. If the past is any indication, he'll probably arrange it so that he can't be located."

Mrs. Lehman sighed. "I'm thankful that we have room. We don't usually get them four at a time. It's hard to believe that child took charge of bringing them here."

She spoke as though Ethan were invisible, and he listened with growing apprehension. They would be allowed to stay tonight, but would they be sent away tomorrow? There were a lot of children around the tables in the dining room. What if they only had room for some of the Cooper family?

No, Ethan decided. *If we can't all stay, I'll take everyone back home.* How this was to be accomplished, he didn't know, but his mind was made up. They had already lost half their family. Nothing was going to separate the rest of them.

Mr. Lehman smiled at Ethan as he stood in front of the desk. "Well, young man, I hear that you've brought your brothers and sister to the Briars by yourself. That was a long trip to make alone."

"Yes, sir," Ethan answered. "But I can take care of them. They depend on me. I'll see that they behave if you'll let us stay."

"Certainly you may stay," Mr. Lehman assured him, "and you'll have help looking after them. Now, you've had a long day. Bert will show you where you'll sleep, and tomorrow we'll get better acquainted."

The long room in which the older boys slept was furnished with a cot and a small cupboard for each child. Ethan was assigned a bed next to Bert, who seemed delighted to have a new friend his own age.

"I'll show you around tomorrow," Bert promised. "This place is pretty nice when you ain't got no family to stay with."

Ethan fell asleep at once.

Several hours later, though, he awoke with a start and studied the strange room. The beds on his side held junior boys. On the opposite wall, five older boys' beds were lined up. Simon and Will weren't in this room. *If they wake*, Ethan thought, *they'll be frightened.* Neither one had ever slept alone in a bed.

Carefully Ethan padded across the hallway to the little boys' room. There he found that Simon had crawled into bed with Will. Ethan pulled the covers over both of them. For tonight they were taken care of.

Chapter Four

EUGENIA QUINCY'S
SUDDEN FANCY

Mrs. Eugenia Quincy shifted restlessly in her pew. She wished that Patterson, her husband, wouldn't insist on attending this simple little chapel every Sunday. There was a perfectly beautiful church in town that was so much more respectable. The wheezy pump organ here was highly inferior to the magnificent instrument at St. Jerome's. And the people … well, she wouldn't even think about the people. No one in her social set would dream of worshipping in a place like this.

The subject had come up yesterday evening.

"Patterson, I don't understand why we can't attend St. Jerome's services with all our friends," she had said.

"I know you don't," Patterson had replied. "That's why I've given up trying to explain it to you."

"Really, you are most annoying. You've been offered a position as deacon at St. Jerome's, and you turned it down to usher in that dreary Briarlane chapel! Do you honestly feel that place befits your station in life?"

"Why, yes, my dear. I've attended the chapel since I was a child, and it hasn't hindered my reaching this 'station in life,' as you call it. In fact, I would say that I've been helped tremendously over the years. I owe a great deal to that little church."

"Hmmph. They owe a great deal to you, if you ask me. They certainly couldn't pay the minister if you didn't contribute. Most of the congregation comes from that orphanage, and everyone knows how much money they have. I would think that serving as president of the board at the Briars would be enough sacrifice for you to make."

Patterson had gone back to his paper, but Eugenia hadn't finished speaking her mind.

"I'm certainly in favor of charitable work, but must it be something so … so religious?"

"I would hardly call teaching Christian values to children too religious," her husband replied. "It seems highly superior to having them grow up on the streets."

"Of course I have nothing against good moral training for them. It's right to be interested in their spiritual welfare. But does it have to take over your whole life?"

A glance at his face told Eugenia she had ventured far enough. It was time to back down. "Oh, never mind. You just don't understand how I feel. But we won't discuss it any further."

"Thank you, Eugenia. You don't know how relieved I am to hear that."

And so this Sunday morning, they were seated near the front of the chapel as the children and staff from the Home filed into their seats across the aisle. Eugenia watched them listlessly, as she did each week. The boys wore denim pants and white shirts, and the girls were attired in light-blue dresses covered with crisp white pinafores. Each child resembled the others. She wondered idly if they had individual names at least.

Suddenly Eugenia sat up and clutched her husband's arm. "Look at that perfectly gorgeous child! The one sitting next to Matron Daly. I haven't seen him before. Does he belong there?"

Patterson squinted toward the group. "That must be one of the new children who came last week. George Lehman mentioned that four more arrived. All one family, I think."

The congregation rose at that moment to begin the service, and Eugenia could say nothing more. But she couldn't take her eyes off the sturdy child. His dark hair lay in waves across his forehead, and his wide gaze took in his new surroundings. When the organ began to play, his attention was riveted on it.

As she watched the boy throughout the service, Eugenia daydreamed. After twelve years of marriage, she and Patterson had no children. This was of little concern to Eugenia, for her life seemed complete with the social affairs that filled her days. As the wife of Briarlane's foremost judge and mistress of the most elegant house in town, Eugenia spent her time at literary-club meetings, fund-raising activities, teas, and parties.

Now it occurred to her that a child like that could enhance her position in Briarlane. Certainly none of her friends had one like him. Their children tended to be noisy, fussy, and ill-mannered. She pictured herself accompanied about town by this small object of perfection. He would be dressed in the latest fashion in a white suit and shoes that buttoned up the sides. He would walk quietly beside her and greet her friends politely. She would see that he had the latest books and toys to entertain him.

By the time the service ended, Eugenia Quincy had mentally embarked upon motherhood and was enjoying her new standing in town.

It seemed to take forever to bow to the other parishioners and wait for Patterson to finish visiting with all his friends. At last they were seated in their limousine and headed for home.

"Patterson, I must have that little boy!"

Her husband turned a startled gaze in her direction. "You must have what?"

"The child who has come to the Briars," Eugenia said impatiently. "The one I pointed out to you before the service. I want you to see about getting him immediately."

He regarded her as though she had taken leave of her senses. "Eugenia, you can't be serious! You know nothing about that child. We aren't acquainted with his background or his family. We don't even know that he's available for adoption. How have you reached this decision when you've only seen him for less than an hour—and that from across the church?"

"I know what I want when I see it," Eugenia replied firmly. "And I want that boy."

Patterson shook his head as if he couldn't believe it. "I propose that we have a quiet dinner before we continue this discussion. I need time to digest what I've already heard."

Eugenia knew by the set of his chin that this would be the final word on the matter until he brought it up again, so she settled into her corner of the car to plan her next move. This might be more difficult than she had envisioned. Patterson could be quite determined when he chose to be.

By the time Eugenia joined her husband on the veranda that afternoon, she was confident that her arguments were sensible and well thought out. She was prepared to answer any objections he might bring forth. She relaxed in her cushioned rocker and bent her head demurely over her embroidery, the picture of patience.

After a lengthy silence, Patterson spoke. "Now, suppose you tell me your reasons for wishing to bring a child into the house at this time?"

It wasn't the way she had expected the conversation to begin. Eugenia hadn't explored that aspect of the situation. There was no reason. She simply had been taken by the handsome little boy and wanted him for her own. But caution told her that this explanation wouldn't satisfy her husband. Perhaps, she admitted to herself, she was bored and needed a new interest in life. She probably wouldn't do well to divulge that information either. What reason would sound logical enough to bring Patterson around to her way of thinking?

"Well?"

"Why, any child has a better chance in life in a home with two parents than in an institution, don't you think? And especially a home that can offer him the advantages we could afford." Eugenia warmed to her subject and hastened on. "The upper floor could be turned into a nursery and schoolroom. I will find a competent woman to take care of him, and he will be a lot of company for us."

"I wasn't aware that you felt the need for more company, my dear. I've been on the board of trustees at the Home for ten years, and you've never expressed an interest in taking one of those children into your care. On the contrary, you've avoided any contact with them. Isn't that so?"

Eugenia felt the color rise in her cheeks. "Well, yes. But they are quite common children. One can't just pick a child off the streets and …" She was backed into a corner, at a loss to explain why this child had taken her fancy or why she felt that she must have him. But Eugenia Quincy was not one to give up without a fight. If this approach didn't work, she would try another.

"I believe we had better give the subject more thought," Patterson said. "Before one takes on the responsibility of a child, there must be compelling reasons for doing so."

Eugenia said no more, but she was fully committed to pursuing the matter on her own. Let her husband do the thinking. She would act.

Chapter Five

ETHAN LEARNS THE RULES

"Come on, Ethan. Can't you move any faster?" Bert's freckled face was anxious as he watched Ethan tying his shoes. "I can hear everyone in the dining room. Hurry! You can make your bed later."

The boys raced down the big staircase and slipped into their seats just as Matron bowed her head to pray. It had taken Ethan a few days to realize that no one ate the good food at mealtime until someone thanked the Lord for it. He wondered why they thanked God when they worked so hard to grow it.

"I don't know," Bert said when Ethan mentioned it. "Maybe because God makes it rain. I guess we can't do that."

Bert had undertaken the job of teaching Ethan the fine art of weeding the garden. "You have to turn the hoe over. You can't cut anything with that side. Ain't you never used a hoe before?"

Ethan admitted that he had not. The few things grown on the Cooper land were weeded by hand. Neither had he fed animals or picked fruit. But now he was being introduced to farm life, and he found that he liked it.

The two rows assigned to them looked long. Ethan surveyed them carefully. "Maybe we can do some weeding now and then finish after we play ball," he suggested.

Bert shook his head. "Nope. That won't work. Mr. Lehman or Otis will check to see what we did. Otis runs the farm, and he knows what everyone is doing. We have to finish our jobs first. That's a rule."

Ethan hadn't lived by that kind of rule before. He did what Pa ordered him to do when he couldn't stay out of Pa's way. Sometimes he was punished whether he obeyed or not. As he chopped weeds now, he remembered the stinging blows on his legs from Pa's strap when he didn't hurry back from town fast enough with Pa's beer. Ethan hadn't seen anyone strapped here.

A sudden shriek from the direction of the barnyard caused Ethan to drop his hoe and run. "That was Simon!" he yelled.

By the time Ethan reached the fence, Otis had the little boy in his arms. In the pen, a hog was pushing his huge snout against the wire.

Simon sobbed loudly. "He bit me! He bit me!"

"He didn't bite you, kid." Otis soothed him. "He thought you had something in your hand to feed him, and he put out his tongue." Otis set Simon back on the ground. "If I was you, I wouldn't try giving chicken feed to the hog anymore. He probably thought your hand was part of the bargain."

Simon clung to Ethan for a moment and then rubbed his wet face with grimy hands.

"He's too big for you to feed, Simon," Ethan told him. "Stick with the chickens. When you get through, come over where I am, and I'll let you help me weed."

"I never had no brother," Bert said as he and Ethan went back to work. "Did you always take care of yours?"

"Yep. I'm pretty good at it too," Ethan boasted. "Ma always had a baby to take care of, so she depended on me. I'll look after them until they grow up, I guess."

For the first time in his life, Ethan wasn't required to keep a watchful eye on the younger children. The habit was hard to break, however. Ethan never ate a meal without checking to see that Alice and Will and Simon were in their places.

One morning Matron Daly stopped Ethan as he left the dining room. "Ethan, you didn't make your bed again this morning."

"Oh, I forgot. I meant to go back and do it."

"That happens too often," Matron said sternly. "You can't go out with the others until it's done. Go to your room and take care of the bed, and then wait there until I come up to inspect it."

Ethan trudged up the stairs and into the big, empty bedroom. There was no reason he couldn't just straighten his bed at night before he got back in it. Ma had never been fussy about making beds.

Slowly he patted the covers in place and then sat on the end of his cot to wait for Matron. He could hear the boys playing under the window and knew they had chosen sides without him. He sighed loudly.

Across the room the beds belonging to the older boys were neatly made and in straight rows, he noticed. He hadn't had anything to do with the big boys except to watch them from afar, but he knew each of them by name. Riley always spoke kindly to him, and his bed was directly across from Ethan's. The next bed belonged to Hugh.

Something on the floor between the beds caught Ethan's eye, and he got up to investigate. It was a picture. He sat on Riley's bed and studied it. The face that gazed back at him was beautiful. Soft hair and smiling eyes made Ethan think of Ma, and suddenly he was overcome with homesickness.

Before he could put the picture down, a big kid grabbed the back of his collar. "Hey! What're you doing on my bed?"

Ethan looked into the face of Riley Walter. "N-nothin'," Ethan stuttered.

But Riley wasn't listening. His angry glance had gone to the picture in Ethan's hand. "Where did you get that? Have you been in my cupboard?"

Ethan shook his head. "It was on the floor."

"It didn't get on the floor by itself," Riley insisted. "I've found my cupboard open before, but I never caught anyone at it." He shook Ethan by the shirt. "Don't you know better than to get into other people's things?"

Ethan nodded wordlessly.

"What else you got that doesn't belong to you?" Riley demanded. "Stand up here and let me look." Quickly he examined one of Ethan's pockets and pulled out the watchcase. "Where'd you get this from?"

"It's mine. I found it in the field at home," Ethan replied in a small voice.

"Sure you did, kid. You never found no watch in a field."
Riley snapped open the lid and looked at the picture. His face
softened. "Who's this? Your ma?"

Ethan nodded again.

"Well, I believe that all right. But I'm not sure you didn't
pick up this watchcase from someone. Here—you take the picture, and I'll just hold on to the case until I find out who lost
it. What else you got in your pockets?" Riley poked his hand
into Ethan's other pocket and came up with the nickel that the
motorman had returned to Ethan.

"Don't tell me you found this in the field too? How come a
kid your age has this much money?" Riley eyed the younger boy
with suspicion. "Maybe I better talk to Mr. Lehman about you.
We don't go for this kind of stuff around here."

Ethan's lip quivered. What if Mr. Lehman sent him away?
"I didn't steal it, honest." He gulped. "But you can have it if you
want."

Riley dropped Ethan's arm. "Naw, I won't keep it. But I'm
going to check around. You better not have stolen it or you're in
big trouble. Now after this, you stay out of my cupboard, hear?"

Ethan blushed, and Riley disappeared down the stairway
after tucking the watchcase into his overalls. Swiping a tear,
Ethan pushed Ma's picture into the far corner of his cupboard
and sat down once more to wait for Matron. Riley would never

trust him after this, and Ethan hadn't even done anything wrong. It wasn't fair. Riley had probably pulled the picture out himself and hadn't notice it fall to the ground. But it wouldn't do to tell anyone about it, Ethan knew. He would simply have to keep out of Riley's way.

Matron Daly entered the room and smiled as she checked the bed. "That's more like it. The Lord is pleased with us when we do our work well."

"You mean the Lord cares how I made my bed?" Ethan was doubtful.

"Of course. The Bible says we should do everything as unto the Lord. That means keeping things neat. Come on down to the laundry with me and bring the boys' clothes back up here. Then you can go out and play."

Ethan followed Matron downstairs and waited patiently as she loaded his arms with clean shirts and underwear. As he trudged back up to the big room, he determined that he wouldn't leave his bed unmade in the future. He was wasting valuable time that could be spent outdoors.

As he neared the room, Ethan heard a cupboard door open and shut. He stopped in the hallway and listened. Another click convinced him that someone was in the bedroom. Everyone was supposed to be outside. Who could it be? Ethan peered cautiously through the doorway.

Hugh. Ethan didn't know much about him, but he did know that Hugh was a bully. He often threatened the younger boys and made them take over some of his chores. So far Ethan had managed to avoid him. He certainly didn't want Hugh to see him now. Quickly he dropped the clothes on the nearest bed and ran to the stairway.

"What took you so long?" Bert asked when Ethan arrived at the field where the boys were playing. "We need another guy on our side."

As the game went on, Ethan worried about what he had seen. Riley had been right. Someone was going through the cupboards. Ethan wondered whether he should report Hugh. If the other boy hadn't seen him, he wouldn't know who had told. Ethan decided to ask Bert for advice.

"Would you tell Matron if you saw someone going through the cupboards?" Ethan said in a low voice.

"Like who?"

"Well, one of the bigger kids."

"Are you crazy?" Bert stared at Ethan. "Want to get your head cracked? Just pretend you don't even see the big guys. It's safer that way."

Ethan pondered the advice as he helped to clear the tables after supper. Maybe it was best to forget the whole thing. He didn't want to be blamed for everything that was missing, though. Maybe he could pray about it. If the Lord was interested in how he made his bed, He might care about this, too. Ethan would remember this when he said his prayers at bedtime.

As Ethan left the dining room, a rough hand pulled him into a corner.

Hugh made a fist and glared at him. "You forget what you saw this morning and keep your mouth shut if you know what's good for you," the big boy snarled. "Bad things happen to kids who blab about stuff that don't concern them. You understand?"

Ethan swallowed hard and nodded.

"You better. I can tell Mr. Lehman that I saw you going through our belongings. He'll believe me, 'cause I've been here longer than you have."

Ethan felt sick. This was the second time today that he had been threatened with someone talking to Mr. Lehman about him. What would happen to the others if he were sent away? Ethan couldn't risk it. He would keep quiet.

"I'm not going to tell, honest."

"Good thing," Hugh warned. "You know what'll happen if you do."

∾

For several days Ethan had a knot in his stomach. Whenever he saw Hugh staring at him, he would look away quickly and pretend not to notice.

One afternoon Ethan was sitting on the steps waiting for Bert. Idly he watched Alice as she played dolls with the other girls.

A voice startled him. "That redheaded one is your sister, isn't she? I bet you wouldn't want anything to happen to her." It was Hugh.

Ethan jumped up, fists clenched. "If you ever touch my sister, you ... you'll be sorry!" he shouted. As Hugh's mouth dropped open in surprise, Ethan turned and raced toward the barn.

Chapter Six

EUGENIA VISITS THE BRIARS

Eugenia Quincy studied her reflection in the hall mirror and pronounced it good. She needed to look her best this morning to accomplish the task before her. Satisfied that there was no visible flaw in her appearance, she opened the big front door of her home.

"I'm leaving, Greta," she called to the housekeeper. "I may not be home for lunch, so don't prepare anything."

Stepping carefully into the limousine, Eugenia leaned back against the soft cushions and took a deep breath. If all went according to plan, she would lunch with Patterson and divulge her good news. There was no reason to think that her plan wouldn't succeed. She had never failed yet.

"I want to go out to the Briars, Gridley," she said. "And I'd like you to wait for me."

"Yes, ma'am." The driver didn't so much as twitch an eyebrow to indicate surprise at the destination. Surely he was well aware of Mrs. Quincy's aversion to the orphanage, but it wasn't his place to speculate on the reason for this trip.

As the car purred toward the edge of town, Eugenia reviewed the strategy she had planned. Although she wasn't well acquainted with the director of the home, Mr. Lehman had always treated her with courtesy and deference. There would surely be no difficulty in persuading him to agree with her point of view. If necessary she could mention that Patterson ... that Patterson what?

She could hardly say that she had come with her husband's blessing, since Patterson knew nothing about her visit and almost certainly wouldn't have blessed it if he had. Oh well. Once he had gotten used to the idea, Patterson would go along with her decision.

The big car drew up before the archway at the Briars, and Gridley opened the door for Eugenia. With a shudder, she peered up at the sign proclaiming Briarlane Christian Children's Home and then walked briskly toward the door. She would have much preferred that Mr. Lehman come to her as her dressmaker did, but she was forced to admit that this was a somewhat different situation.

The door was opened by a boy who appeared to be polishing the wood panels as his morning chore. Eugenia glanced at him and drew her skirts higher around her as she swept into the hallway.

"Please tell Mr. Lehman that Mrs. Quincy desires to see him," she announced.

"Yes, ma'am." The boy scurried off, leaving Eugenia standing by the door. She tapped her foot impatiently. She might at least have been offered a chair while she waited. This was an example of the kind of child that was sheltered here, she thought. Certainly no training in social graces. All the more reason her errand was an important one.

To Eugenia's gratification, Mr. Lehman himself came out to greet her. "Mrs. Quincy. What a pleasant surprise. Won't you come in?"

He ushered her into the shabby but comfortable office. A wall of books, a desk piled high with folders and papers, and several chairs completed the scene. He pulled the most comfortable seat toward the desk for his visitor.

Eugenia scanned the room with barely concealed distaste. Was this where Patterson conducted the board meetings each month? Why in the world had he not done something about the appearance of the place?

George Lehman's voice interrupted her thoughts. "What can I do for you, Mrs. Quincy?"

Eugenia turned her brightest smile in his direction. She might as well dispense with the small talk and proceed directly to the point. The place was depressing, and she had no desire to stay any longer than necessary.

"I understand that you have recently taken in four new children," she said.

Mr. Lehman nodded. "Yes, the Cooper children."

"I want the youngest one."

George Lehman seemed unable to hide his astonishment. "I beg your pardon?"

Why do men have to be so slow-witted? Eugenia thought irritably. He was acting just like Patterson. What was so hard to understand?

"I … we …. want to adopt the youngest one," she repeated with impatience. "What is his name?"

"William," Mr. Lehman answered automatically, "but—"

"I'll call him Reginald," Eugenia declared. "Can Matron get him ready immediately?"

Mr. Lehman leaned back in his chair and studied his visitor. "I'm sorry, Mrs. Quincy, but I'm afraid that will be impossible."

"I don't understand."

"The Cooper children won't be available for adoption until the father is located," the man explained. "If and when that occurs, they will all go together."

"Together! Ridiculous! Who is going to take four children at one time? Your main concern is placing children in good homes, isn't it? What is the reason for all these silly rules?"

"The Home is under state regulation, Mrs. Quincy. Even if I wanted to separate the Cooper children, I couldn't do so without the consent of the family."

Eugenia was no longer wearing her brightest smile. She was unaccustomed to being denied anything, and she found the situation most wearisome. As she smoothed her gloves in her lap, her mind tackled the problem. She didn't want to use the last weapon in her arsenal, but there seemed to be no alternative.

"Mr. Quincy has given much to this institution over the years. I'm afraid I shall have to ask him to withdraw his support unless …" Her meaning was clear.

"We appreciate Mr. Quincy's generous gifts," Mr. Lehman said carefully, "but in this instance, there is nothing I can do. I'm sorry."

"I expect we'll see about that, won't we?" Eugenia rose and strode haughtily toward the door.

George Lehman hurried to open it for her.

"Good day, Mr. Lehman. You will be hearing from me again."

I'm sure I will, George Lehman thought as he watched Eugenia leave.

The sound of the big front door closing signaled her departure. Watching out the office window, he followed the angry woman with his gaze as she sailed down the path and entered her limousine.

When she was gone, George felt as though he had done battle with the Furies.

Bert wasted no time locating Ethan in the barn, where he was sweeping the floor.

"You can't guess what I just heard," he whispered hoarsely, "up there by the office."

Visions of both Riley and Hugh approaching Mr. Lehman about him held Ethan speechless. He stared at the freckles on Bert's face and clutched his broom for support.

"A fancy lady in a huge car is going to take Will away. I heard her tell Mr. Lehman."

Ethan had difficulty switching his thinking from the threat he'd been anticipating to a threat unimaginable, and he continued to stare at Bert.

"Didn't you hear me? I said—"

But Ethan had dropped the broom and grabbed Bert's skinny arm. "What lady? What car? Did she take Will?"

"Ow! Leggo! I didn't do nothin'! No. She said she'd be back." Bert rubbed his arm and backed off. "I thought you'd want to know."

"She can't do that," Ethan declared. "They won't let her take him, will they?"

Bert regained his composure. "Look, Ethan, this here is an orphanage. That's the kind of stuff they do—get homes for kids like us. Well, maybe not us," Bert reconsidered, "but little kids like Will, or blonde, curly-haired girls."

Ethan felt a moment of relief. So Alice would be safe. Her hair was red and as straight as it could be.

He sank onto a bale of hay. "She can't have Will. I won't let her. Nobody can unless they take all of us."

Bert sat beside him. "How you goin' to stop her?" he asked.

Ethan's shoulders drooped as he peered at his friend. "I don't know. What shall I do?"

Bert chewed thoughtfully on a straw. "Looks to me like this is serious enough to pray about," he offered. "You ever prayed besides 'Now I lay me down to sleep'?"

Ethan shook his head. "Not much. I prayed that Ma would get better, but she didn't. I prayed that Russell would let me stay home, but here I am."

Ethan thought of all that had happened since he'd forgotten to make his bed and Matron had told him that the Lord was interested in how he did his work. It looked like that was all the Lord was interested in. First Riley and then Hugh had threatened him, and now Will was in danger. For someone who hadn't had much practice, it looked like he was collecting a lot of things to pray about.

Come to think of it, Ethan told himself, *you don't seem to be very good at praying.*

Perhaps he'd better begin to make some plans of his own. "Who is this lady with the car?" he asked Bert.

"She said her name was Mrs. Quincy." Bert glanced at his friend. "And that she'd call Will 'Reginald' when she took him home."

Ethan was disgusted. "Reginald! What kind of name is that? Anyway, Ma named him William, and she can't change that. You've got to help me think of some way to keep her from taking him."

"I don't know." Bert looked doubtful. "I've noticed that grown-ups pretty much do what they want when it comes to kids."

This fact hadn't escaped Ethan's attention either. But when it came to the safety of his little brother, he was ready to fight even grown-ups. "I'll find someplace to hide him," he announced.

"Where you going to hide someone that big?" Bert wanted to know. "Your cupboard is too small, and they clean under the beds."

"What are you planning to hide, kid?" Hugh had appeared out of nowhere.

When neither younger boy answered, he repeated his question.

"N-nothing," Ethan stammered. "We—I—didn't take anything."

"So how come you need a place to hide it?"

"He wants to hide—" Bert began, but a sharp poke from Ethan ended the explanation.

Hugh stared at the boys, but neither said any more. "Won't talk, huh? Well, don't forget that I'll be watching you, and you know what happens to kids who don't mind their own business."

When Hugh had disappeared out the barn door, Bert turned to Ethan. "What's the matter with him? What'd he mean about minding our own business?"

"I guess he doesn't want us to talk about him." Ethan shrugged.

"I don't want to talk about him," Bert declared. "I don't even want to think about him. We got enough problems of our own."

Ethan nodded in agreement. He couldn't tell Bert that Hugh was one of the problems.

As the days went by and no one carried Will off, Ethan began to relax. Bert had probably misunderstood the conversation he'd overheard. Besides, there were a lot of other things to claim Ethan's attention.

Chapter Seven

EUGENIA TRIES AGAIN

Eugenia Quincy returned to the orphanage after giving Mr. Lehman a few days to rethink his position. She entered the office with a cheerful spirit and a determined step. Mr. Lehman seated her and waited politely for her to open the conversation.

"I hope you have reconsidered your decision about the young Cooper child," she said. "You do know the advantages we have to offer him. Mr. Quincy is in a position to expedite the adoption, and I would like to have it taken care of at once."

"Perhaps I didn't make myself clear when we spoke earlier," George Lehman replied. "This isn't a matter within my jurisdiction. Any living parent must be located and must give permission for an adoption to take place. We haven't located

Mr. Cooper yet. Also, as I mentioned, the older children in the family don't want the younger ones separated. We will honor their wishes."

Unbelievable! Eugenia thought. *Here is a man who doesn't realize the danger of opposing me. Well, he soon will.*

Eugenia Quincy continued to smile as she sat in George Lehman's office. But her eyes flashed a warning that George didn't fail to note.

"I see," she continued. "I'm sure that if you give it careful thought, you'll find that there are loopholes in every situation, even this one. In the meantime, there could be no objection to my taking the child for a few days to get him acquainted with his future home, could there? I'd appreciate it if you would ask Matron to get him ready at once. I have errands to complete, and I'm running late."

George was becoming impatient with this woman. In deference to her husband's position, he had to treat her with civility, but he might as well be talking to a tree stump. She obviously hadn't heard a word he'd said.

"I'm sorry, Mrs. Quincy. We appreciate your interest in Will, but the boy is too young to be away from the people he knows. It wouldn't be wise to upset him that way."

With those final words, George arose. As far as he was concerned, the matter was settled. But as he again watched Mrs.

Quincy march toward her car, the uncomfortable feeling that it was most certainly not settled stayed with him.

Eugenia sighed at dinner and put her fork down.

"You aren't eating, my dear. Are you not feeling well?" Patterson asked.

"I'm fine," she replied. "Just restless. There's not much going on. I need something to occupy my time." She glanced furtively at her husband, but he had gone on with his dinner and didn't appear to take the hint she had given him.

"I'm very busy at this time, or I would arrange for us to get away," Patterson said finally. "I'm afraid I can't spare Gridley right now to go with you either. Why don't you take Clara and run up to the lake for a few days? You could drive the small car. Perhaps I can join you later in the week."

This wasn't what she'd had in mind. However, her voice was even as she answered him. "Thank you, dear. I'll think about that."

As she wandered discontentedly around the house that evening, the suggestion became more attractive. It had been a long time since she'd had to fight this hard for something she wanted. The longer it took, the more determined she was to have it. She needed to get away to think this through.

Her mind made up, Eugenia called Clara to her room. The dark-haired, young servant appeared promptly.

"Clara, pack bags for you and me to go to the summer house. I'd like to leave early tomorrow morning."

"Yes, mum. Will the mister be going?"

"No, there will be just the two of us. Ask Greta to prepare some food for us to take."

"How much food, mum?"

"Oh, I don't know." Eugenia waved her away. "Enough for a week at least. Mr. Quincy can bring what we need if I decide to stay longer."

Clara departed, and Eugenia threw herself down on the chaise lounge. Was she the only one in this house who could make a decision about anything? At least she was sure of one thing. She would have a foolproof scheme for getting that child before she returned home.

Chapter Eight

WILL GOES FOR A RIDE

One bright morning Otis made an announcement after breakfast.

"Whitewash day, boys. Bert, Philip, Ethan, and Billy—work on the henhouses. You older fellows come with me."

"What are we going to do?" Ethan asked as he trotted along with the others. "What is whitewash?"

"Paint," Bert explained. "All the outbuildings get cleaned up with it once a year. I guess it kills the bugs. Makes 'em look better, too."

"The bugs?"

"Naw, silly. Didn't you have a henhouse or pigsty or nothin' at your place?"

Ethan recalled the few scrawny chickens that scratched around the Cooper yard. They had roosted in the trees at night. He had to admit he remembered nothing that was painted.

It didn't take him long to enter wholeheartedly into the project. Paint flew everywhere as the boys happily sloshed big brushes against the wood. An occasional jab at one another as they worked side by side seemed like a good idea, and it wasn't long until the boys and buildings had received a generous coat of whitewash.

It was Ethan who noticed the hog snoring peacefully in the dusty pen. "He could use some cleaning up," Ethan said to Bert. "And you know he has bugs."

Bert looked doubtful. "I don't know if we're supposed to paint hogs. Maybe it isn't good for them."

"It doesn't hurt us," Ethan argued, "and his hide is tougher than ours. Come on. Let's try it."

"You try it," Bert decided. "He might wake up and not like it. Get in the pen, and I'll hand you the paint."

It took only a moment for Ethan to scramble over the fence and into the pigsty.

"I'd stay behind him if I were you," Bert advised. "If he opens his eyes, he won't see you first off." He looked nervous as Ethan approached the big animal with the pail and brush. "If he starts to get up, come out of there quick," Bert added. "He could knock you down with his snout."

Ethan eyed the hog. "He does look a lot bigger in here than he did out there," he admitted. "If he wakes up, I'll get away."

Ethan needn't have worried. The hog was dead to the world and didn't move as Ethan began at his tail and moved up the huge side with the paintbrush. Bert hung on the fence and gazed wide-eyed until Ethan reached the hog's ears. Then there came a snuffle and a snort, and the earth trembled.

"Whoa!" Bert shouted. "He's turning over, Ethan. You better move!"

Ethan jumped back, but he wasn't quick enough. Without opening an eye, the huge beast flipped to the other side and flattened Ethan to the ground.

"Hey, look at that!" Bert marveled. "He didn't even wake up, and you can paint the other side."

Ethan wiped the dust off his face and glared at Bert. "Not much, I can't. He's sitting on me."

There was silence while Bert took this in. "You mean you can't get up out of there?"

"My leg's under him, and I sure can't shove him over again. Now what are we going to do?"

"Won't do any good for me to poke him," Bert determined. "I'll run and get Otis. Stay right there."

It's not like I could go anywhere, Ethan thought as he considered his dismal situation. *I just hope this hog stays asleep.*

Otis soon arrived with a rake, and after much prodding with the handle, he got the animal onto his feet. Then Otis scooped Ethan off the ground and ran for the fence.

"I never told you boys to whitewash the inside of the pigsty," he said sternly. "It's a wonder you weren't killed."

"We weren't painting the pigsty, Otis," Bert informed him. "We were painting the hog."

"Painting the hog?" Otis exclaimed in disbelief. "If that animal hadn't been so full and so sound asleep, he'd of ate you alive. What in tarnation did you want to do that for?"

"Ethan thought it would kill the bugs," Bert explained.

"And he sure had a lot of room to look better. He's one heavy pig." Ethan rubbed his leg and hopped around on it.

"If you hadn't landed in one of those holes he's dug out, he'd a-busted that leg in two," Otis told him. "Brush as much of the muck off as you can and go on up to the house. I'm sure Matron will be glad to see you."

Otis stomped back to the barn, and Bert translated the message. "He really means she *won't* be glad to see you. Matron doesn't like messes."

Bert thought for a moment. Then his face lit up. "I know! We'll go down to the stream, and you can splash around with your clothes on. That'll wash 'em out, and by the time we go up to dinner, you'll be dry. Matron won't have to know what you did."

Within seconds the boys raced off to the stream running through the farmland. Since they were there, they figured they might as well both enjoy a swim.

"Oww!" Ethan yelled. "This is cold!"

"Keep moving fast," Bert instructed. "It'll take a while to get rid of all that dirt and paint."

Ready to depart, Eugenia Quincy was attired in a long driving coat, her large hat secured firmly with a gauzy scarf. Gridley fastened the bags to the back of the car, settled a big wicker basket beside Clara in the backseat, and stepped back. Eugenia took her place behind the wheel and drew on her gloves.

"Have a safe trip, madam."

Eugenia nodded. "Thank you, Gridley."

The car chugged out of the circular drive. The fifteen-mile trip covered roads on which the travelers were likely to meet nothing more than an occasional horse, and the little car didn't begin to reach the speed of the limousine.

The route to the lake took Eugenia past the Briars. Though she usually ignored the Home as she passed, this morning she recalled with annoyance her unsatisfactory conversation with George Lehman. She really should report the man to Patterson for his insubordination … but that would mean telling her husband what she'd been up to.

As the car approached the arched sign over the entrance, Eugenia slowed down and regarded it with distaste. Stubborn man!

All of a sudden, she stopped the car, and Clara was forced to lunge for the basket before it slid to the floor.

"Oh! What is it, mum?"

Eugenia didn't answer but stepped down from the high seat and walked to the fence that surrounded the lawn. There stood a small boy staring with obvious delight at the vehicle in the road.

Eugenia smiled at him. "Hello, there. Do you like that car?"

The boy nodded. "Pretty car!"

Eugenia surveyed the yard and the building. There was no one in sight. "Would you like a ride in the pretty car?"

His eyes lit up, and he nodded vigorously.

Eugenia leaned over the fence and picked him up. Swiftly she deposited the little boy on Clara's lap in the backseat. Before the girl could even speak, the car was moving again.

"Oh, mum!" Clara gasped. "What have you done? You can't just take him! What will the Home say?"

"I know what I'm doing, Clara. Just hold on to him."

"Oh, mum!" Clara wailed. "They'll be after us!"

"Don't be ridiculous. We'll have him back in a few days. There are so many children running around in there that they'll never miss him." What sounded like a sob from the backseat irritated Eugenia. "For goodness' sake, Clara, stop that sniffling! If you must know, I've already talked to Mr. Lehman about taking the boy."

It seemed unnecessary at this point to add that Mr. Lehman had refused permission. She didn't need a terror-stricken servant on her hands for the rest of the week.

Little Will Cooper shrieked and jumped with delight as the car gathered speed and the wind rushed through his hair. Clara had her hands full keeping him from falling over the side in his excitement.

Chapter Nine

ETHAN LEARNS TO TRUST

By the time Ethan and Bert emerged from the river, they were shivering and blue with cold. Suddenly a meeting with Matron didn't seem like such a bad thing to look forward to.

"I don't care what happens," Ethan declared. "I'm going in to get some other clothes. Come on, let's run." The boys raced across the field toward the house.

"If we go in through the kitchen and up the back stairs, maybe no one will see us," Bert said, panting. "The cook will be too busy to notice."

As they neared the back steps, Ethan slowed down and grabbed Bert's arm. "Oh no. Look who's on the porch waiting for us."

It was Hugh. The older boy grinned and sauntered toward them. "What happened to you guys? Fall in the horse trough? I wouldn't go in there if I were you. Matron is in the kitchen." He looked directly at Ethan. "She's looking for you. And so is your little sister."

Ethan forgot about the water dripping from the legs of his overalls and the cold, wet hair plastered to his head. He charged blindly into Hugh with both fists beating furiously. "What did you do to my sister?" he shouted. "Did you hurt her? Where is she?"

Bert grabbed the back of Ethan's shirt and tried to drag him away from Hugh. "Hey! What are you doing? Cut it out, Ethan!"

Hugh held Ethan at arm's length. "Take it easy, kid. I didn't do nothin' to your sister. I just heard her yelling for you. And I heard Matron ask where you were. You'd better go back to the barn until you dry off a little. Whatever she wants you for will be twice as bad if she sees you looking like that."

Hugh's advice came too late. Just then Matron opened the door and stepped out onto the porch. She spied the two soaked boys standing in the yard.

"Oh my," she exclaimed. "Look at you. I hope Will doesn't look that bad." She surveyed the area and then her gaze returned to Ethan. "He was with you, wasn't he?"

Ethan backed off from Hugh and stared at her blankly.

Matron hurried down the steps and shook Ethan's shoulder. "Wasn't Will with you? Where is he?"

"No, ma'am," Bert answered for him. "Nobody was with us. We've been—"

But Matron had swiftly reentered the house.

Ethan seemed rooted to the spot until Bert yanked at him. "Come on. Let's find Alice. She knows where Will is."

"I think Ethan knows where he is too," Hugh said. "I heard you talking about hiding something. What else would it be if you ain't stole nothin'? Guess I better go up and tell Mr. Lehman about it. There's several things I could tell him, you know." He stuffed his hands in his pockets and turned away.

"No! No!" Ethan ran after him. "You can't tell him! I never took anything, and I didn't hide anything. I don't know where Will is."

Hugh stopped and tilted his head toward Bert. "Why don't you run and find Alice?" he suggested. "Tell her that Ethan is back here." Bert took off, and Hugh turned back to Ethan. "Well, maybe I will go up to his office and maybe I won't. It all depends."

"Depends on what?" Ethan inquired nervously.

"I could use a little help with something I'm planning." Hugh rubbed his chin. "I might forget what I heard if you was willing to help me." Then he shook his head. "Naw … I probably wouldn't be able to trust you. After all, I did find you sneaking around the bedroom the other day."

Ethan didn't even consider reminding Hugh that he, not Ethan, had been the one sneaking around. Mr. Lehman must not hear anything that would cause him to send Ethan away. But if he had to go, he was determined to take the others with him.

"You can trust me," Ethan insisted. "You can. I'll do anything you say. But I have to find Will first."

Bert and Alice raced toward them, and Hugh turned away again. "I dunno. I'll have to think about it," he said, and then he disappeared around the corner of the house.

Alice grabbed Ethan around the waist. "I can't find Will," she sobbed. "He was playing out there on the grass, and then he was gone. I've called and called him. You have to find him, Ethan. You have to!"

"We will," Ethan assured her. "We'll find him in no time. He's too little to go very far. Where did you see him last?"

Before Alice could answer, Matron reappeared. "Boys, come in this instant and change your clothes. We have enough trouble around here without two cases of pneumonia."

"But Will," Ethan protested. "I have to find Will."

Matron took both boys by the arm and headed for the porch. "No buts. We've got folks looking for him. He's probably fallen asleep out there in the haymow, and he'll be back here before you're dressed. Now get upstairs."

Ethan was in despair. Why did he always have to worry about two things at once? If only he had remembered to make his bed, this never would have happened. He wouldn't have caught Hugh going through the cupboards, and Hugh wouldn't have anything to tell Mr. Lehman.

And why hadn't he kept a better eye on Will? Then, too, what if Otis decided to report that the hog had been painted? How had Ethan gotten himself into so much trouble without even knowing he was doing it?

Bert's voice broke into his dismal thoughts. "Ethan, what if that lady came back in the big car and got Will?"

Ethan had almost forgotten about her. His eyes widened. "No, she couldn't have. We'd have seen her."

"Not from the river," Bert reminded him. "We weren't in sight of the road the whole time."

"We've got to tell someone you heard her say she was going to take him!" Ethan exclaimed. "We can tell Matron, and she'll let Mr. Lehman know."

Bert sat on the edge of the bed with a worried look on his face. "I don't think we can do that, Ethan. I wasn't supposed to hear that, and Matron doesn't like listening in. We'd be in big trouble with Mr. Lehman."

Ethan sank onto his own bed. "Yeah. That's right. We'll have to think of something else."

When Will was nowhere to be found, the rest of the afternoon turned into a frantic search of the grounds around the house. The barn was searched from top to bottom. The older boys walked through the woods calling for Will. By suppertime everyone was tired and discouraged. The only thing that had been found was the little stick horse with the leather strap. It lay beside the fence where its small owner had dropped it.

Ethan had trouble eating his supper, and it was even harder to fall asleep. If Will were out wandering around, he would be frightened and crying. Even if the lady had taken him, he would be lonely and afraid. Ethan rolled over and buried his face in his pillow so none of the boys would awaken and hear him crying.

A gentle hand was laid on his shoulder. "Ethan," Matron said softly, "I came to tell you that everything will be all right. Mr. Lehman will find him. Shall we pray about it together?"

Ethan nodded. When Matron asked the Lord to protect Will and bring him back safely, Ethan wondered if the Lord was really listening. After all, his life had gotten a lot more complicated since he found out that God was interested in him. Was Matron sure that prayers were answered? He figured it might not be a good thing to ask, so he remained silent.

"Ethan, have you heard the story that Jesus told in the Bible about the good shepherd?"

"No."

"Do you want me to tell it to you?"

Ethan nodded again, and Matron settled on the edge of his bed. "There was a man who had a hundred sheep, like the ones out here on the farm," she began. "Every morning he would take them out to the pasture to eat, and he would watch them carefully. Every evening he brought them back to their pen. The shepherd would stand by the gate and count them as they went in. When he had counted one hundred, he would lock the gate and go home for his supper.

"One night the shepherd counted only ninety-nine sheep. He looked around closely, for he knew them all very well, and discovered that the very smallest one was missing. Quickly he locked the gate and then went back to look for the lost sheep. He searched for a long time. He didn't give up, even though it was dark and lonely out in the pasture. Finally, after many hours, he found the little one who had wandered away. The shepherd carried him back and put him in the pen with the others. Then he could go home."

Matron paused. "Jesus told that story because He wants us to know that He is the Good Shepherd, and we are His sheep. He knows about Will. He knows right where Will is. The Good Shepherd wants us to trust Him. Do you think you can do that?"

"I'll try," Ethan said. "I like that story. If someone is taking care of Will, I guess I can sleep."

Matron patted his head and then left. Ethan, comforted, turned over and slept.

Chapter Ten

YES, MR. QUINCY
GETS INVOLVED

The morning after Will's disappearance, Ethan and Bert retreated to the old wagon stored behind the bam. There they sat, bare legs swinging over the tailgate as they pondered the best way to proceed with their day. Aside from Matron's chores, they had been assigned no job for the morning. Everyone was concerned about the missing boy, and the most judicious plan seemed to be to keep out of their way. The older fellows had again been dispatched to the fields and the woods to search.

"The only place no one has looked is the house that lady with the big car came from," Bert remarked finally. "They don't know about that."

"Maybe we should do that ourselves," Ethan suggested. "If we found him there, they'd be so glad, they'd forget to ask how we knew."

Bert's eyes sparkled. "Hey, that's a great idea! Let's do it!"

The boys jumped from the wagon and took off toward the road.

"Where are we going?" Ethan was breathing hard as he tried to keep up with Bert.

At the question, Bert stopped. "I don't know."

"You mean you don't know where she lives?"

"Nope. All I know is she said her name was Mrs. Quincy." Bert looked discouraged for a moment and then brightened. "Shala! She'll know. She's been here since she was little, and she knows everything. We'll ask her."

"You ask her," Ethan said. "I'll wait here for you."

He sank to the ground as Bert sped off. Shala hadn't been overly cordial to him since the day they arrived. She probably wouldn't give him any information if he did ask her.

Bert soon returned with the good news that Shala knew exactly where the Quincy house was. She had demanded to know why Bert was interested.

"The only reason I could think to tell her was that we wanted to see that big car up close. That would be no lie. I would like to look it over, wouldn't you?"

Ethan nodded, and they hurried on their way to the edge of town. Their steps slowed when they came in sight of the house, surrounded by green lawn and trees. It was an awesome sight. A broad porch encircled the entire structure, and wide steps led to the big front doors. Sunlight danced and sparkled from every window, and white paint gleamed in the morning brightness.

"Wow!" Ethan breathed. "That's almost as big as the Briars. I wonder how many kids live here?"

Bert didn't answer. He was frowning as if busy wondering whether they should approach the front door or go around to the back.

"What are we going to say when she comes to the door?" Ethan asked. "Just ask if we can see Will?"

"We better find out if he's here or not. Maybe the one who has door duty today will know."

They pulled the bell, and it seemed a long time before the door opened, revealing a large woman wrapped in a big white apron. She gaped in surprise at the two boys standing before her with dusty, bare feet and overalls cut off at the knee.

"Are you Mrs. Quincy?" Ethan blurted.

"Naw!" Bert tugged at his arm. "That ain't Mrs. Quincy. That's the Matron."

"Now that you have that settled, boys," the woman said, "I'm Greta. What is it you want?"

"We want to see Mrs. Quincy," Bert answered. "We want to ask her something."

"Well, I'm afraid you can't do that," Greta replied. "Mrs. Quincy left town yesterday, and I don't know when she'll be back."

Ethan's shoulders sagged with disappointment. "Did she take Will with her?"

"Will? Who's Will? Clara's the only one who went along."

"Will's my little brother, ma'am. We can't find him, and we heard—"

A sharp poke from Bert's elbow reminded Ethan that they weren't to mention anything they'd heard.

Greta eyed them sharply, her forehead wrinkled in puzzlement. "I'm sorry, boys. I can't help you. I don't know anything about your little brother."

She stepped back into the house, and two dejected boys trudged back to the road. What were they going to do now?

The two unhappy boys sat beside the road to think over their situation. The problem seemed to be bigger than they could handle.

"Matron said that the Good Shepherd knows where Will is," Ethan said. "I wonder why He doesn't tell us?"

"I don't think He talks out loud to people," Bert offered. "In the story, He brought the lost sheep back Himself. So He'll bring Will back too. We might as well go home and wait."

Ethan nodded, but neither boy moved. The sun was warm on their backs, and the breeze carried the smell of new grass and lilacs. After being so sure that they were going to the right place, disappointment seemed to leave them motionless.

"If the lady didn't take Will, who do you suppose did?" Ethan wondered. "Somebody must have. He was too little to go alone."

"I don't know." Bert sighed. "Not a whole lot of people go by our road. Only folks on the way out of town." Bert sat up straighter. "We can go look in town and ask people if they saw him. Someone might have noticed a little boy they hadn't seen before."

Ethan was willing to agree with this theory, and they headed right away for the center of the little town. Horses and buggies were lined up along the main street, and people walked back and forth in front of the stores. The excitement of seeing all this activity slowed the boys down a bit.

"I remember coming past here from the trolley station," Ethan said. "It's better to come this way. You can stop and look in the store windows."

This they did, lingering long over a display of bicycles and toy wagons. They dared not venture inside the stores, since they had no money to spend, but there was much to see from the street.

"Look, Ethan!" Bert grabbed his arm. "There's a lady with a little boy! He looks something like Will!"

Bert pointed across the road, where two figures moved rapidly away from them.

Without looking either way, Ethan darted into the dusty street.

Bert grabbed the straps of Ethan's overalls and yanked him back. "You gotta watch out, or you'll get run down," he warned. "Look what's coming."

A large wagon pulled by a team of horses lumbered by. Buckets hung from the back, and ladders were strapped on the sides. Something that looked like a huge barrel lay in the bed of the wagon. The boys watched in fascination as it passed them in a cloud of dust.

"That's a fire wagon," Bert informed Ethan. "They can come in a hurry if something is burning."

"Did you ever see them do it?" Ethan asked.

"Well, no. We never had a fire out at the Home. We'd probably see it a lot if we lived in town."

"I think I like where I am better," Ethan decided. "There's more stuff to keep us busy."

Suddenly he remembered what they had started out to do. Squinting down the street, he saw that the woman and the little boy had disappeared.

"Come on," Bert said. "If we run, maybe we can catch them."

Several minutes later they slowed down. It was no use. The pair was nowhere in sight. The boys began to walk again.

"I think we've looked everywhere we can," Bert said. "We might as well go back home."

But Ethan was fascinated by the big building closest to them. "That's the seat," he informed Bert.

"The seat of what?"

"I don't know." Ethan shrugged. "That's what the station-master told us. I wonder who lives there?"

Bert surveyed the building. "I don't think anyone does." Men and women were going in and out the front doors. "It looks more like people work there. Nobody seems to be watching who goes in. Want to go see?"

Since he couldn't think of anyplace else to look for Will, Ethan followed Bert through the large doors.

The boys knew better than to enter a closed room, but if a door stood open, they didn't hesitate to stop and look it over from the hallway. An endless number of things seemed to be going on in this building. Typewriters clacked and telephones rang. Young men with bundles of papers hurried by. People entered a big room whose swinging doors revealed long rows of seats and a big desk at the front.

"That looks a little like a school," Bert said, "but there ain't no desks to write on."

"Maybe it's a church where the preacher sits down," Ethan suggested. "But it's sure a lot bigger than our church."

While they stood discussing the possibilities, a smiling woman swung the door open and stepped into the hallway. "Good morning, boys," she said. "Are you looking for someone?"

"Yes, ma'am," Ethan answered promptly. "My brother."

"Does he work here?"

"Oh no, ma'am. He's only two years old. He's lost."

"Two years old!" the lady exclaimed. "What makes you think he might be here? How long has he been lost? Where are your parents?"

The questions came so fast that Ethan was unable to answer. He just stood with his mouth open.

Bert tried, however. "He was lost yesterday. We thought maybe—"

At that moment an impressive-looking man walked out of the big room and stopped to gaze at the dusty, barefoot boys.

"Well, well. What have we here, Miss Clark? Are these friends of yours?"

"I've just met them, sir," Miss Clark replied. "They tell me they've lost a little boy."

"Is that so?" The man fixed his gaze on Ethan and Bert. "Perhaps you'd better tell me about it."

He led the way to an office, and the boys were soon perched uneasily on the edge of chairs in a big room. The man settled behind his desk.

"Now. Let's hear what's going on. Suppose you tell me first where you live."

"At the Briars, sir," Bert answered.

The man blinked. "Briarlane Children's Home?" he asked, looking surprised. "And whom did you say you've lost?"

"My little brother, sir," Ethan said. "Yesterday."

"And what is your name?"

"Ethan. Ethan Cooper."

The man frowned. "Mr. Lehman knows about this, does he?"

"Yes, sir. He's looking for Will now. We thought maybe—" Ethan stopped. He'd better not tell this man their suspicions. They didn't even know who he was. They could get into trouble.

"Shall I see that the boys get back to the Home, Judge Quincy?" Miss Clark asked.

Judge Quincy! Bert and Ethan looked at each other in dismay. That was the name of the lady they were trying to find. If the matron of her house told the judge that they had been there, they were already in trouble.

"No, Miss Clark," Mr. Quincy replied. "Thank you anyway. I believe I'll take them out myself. I'd better look into this matter."

Ethan's shoulders drooped. Would his problems never end? Mr. Lehman would have to know what they had done without permission, and they were no closer to finding Will than before.

Slowly the boys followed Mr. Quincy out of the building. It would be a long walk back to the Home.

Then, to their happy surprise, they found they weren't going to walk. At the rear of the building stood a limousine.

Bert happily exclaimed, "That's the big car, Ethan! The one she came in."

Mr. Quincy appeared perplexed. "You've seen this car before?"

"Oh yes, sir," Bert replied eagerly. "The lady came with this man. Twice." He pointed at the attendant, who looked neither right nor left.

Patterson considered this news as he ushered the two boys into the car. Why had Eugenia—it had to be Eugenia—gone to the Home? Why hadn't she mentioned it to him? Gridley had said nothing about such a trip. But then, Patterson thought, he wouldn't expect the man to. Eugenia had access to the car whenever she wished.

He turned his attention to the excited boys.

"We never rode in a fine car like this before!" Bert exclaimed.

"We never rode in no car before," Ethan corrected him.

"Wait till the guys see us come home like this!"

Then the boys exchanged a glance and both sat back against the seat with sober expressions.

Patterson noticed the sudden quiet and hurried to reassure them. "It's all right, boys. If you're worried about getting into trouble for coming into town, I'll talk to Mr. Lehman when we get there. Perhaps you'd better tell me what you know. When did you say you last saw your little brother?"

"Yesterday. He was there at breakfast. Then we went to paint the henhouses—" Ethan choked.

Bert took up the story. "Then when we got back, Matron said she thought Will was with us. But we hadn't seen him."

Patterson nodded. "So you thought he might have wandered off toward town."

"No, we thought that Mis—" Bert stopped at a glare from Ethan. "That maybe someone took him away, and we'd see him there," Bert finished.

"Chances are he's back by now," Patterson encouraged them. "If not, we'll soon find him, I'm sure."

The car stopped in front of the orphanage gate, and the boys tumbled out. They ran toward the barn to find Otis.

Patterson Quincy walked slowly toward the Home. Several things about this situation disturbed him. How long ago had Eugenia mentioned wanting a child from here? A couple of weeks, he thought. And if he recalled correctly, it was a young Cooper boy that she had specified.

But that was ridiculous. He had convinced her there was no possibility of such a thing, and nothing more had been said about it. That it might be this child who was missing was coincidental. If Eugenia had visited here—twice—there would be an obvious explanation. George Lehman would straighten it out.

Patterson arrived at the door and was admitted into the dim, cool hall. George Lehman soon seated his guest in front of the desk.

Patterson studied the director. "You look worried, George. Anything wrong?"

"Yes, there is. Quite wrong. The youngest of the new family of children has been missing since sometime yesterday. We've carefully searched the house area, the woods, and even the river. There is no sign of him. I sent one of the older boys into town a while ago with a message for you. I don't know how he could have gotten there already."

"Probably hasn't." Patterson then told Mr. Lehman about the two small boys who had delivered the message by accident. "They didn't know who I was. They just wandered into the courthouse. I told them I'd square things with you so they wouldn't be in trouble."

Mr. Lehman smiled slightly. "They won't be punished. I know how worried Ethan has been. The boy is just like a father to the other three, and he's not much older than they are. In fact—"

Mr. Lehman looked distressed.

"Yes?"

"I suspect that the father may have come by and taken the baby with him. We've not been able to locate the man and have no idea what part of the country he may be in. As I explained to your wife, we've done our best to find him so that the children may be released for adoption or returned home. So far we've had no success."

"Mmm, yes." Patterson was troubled. "You say you've talked to Eugenia? Was that about this child who is missing?"

"Why, yes. I thought you knew about it. I didn't mean to divulge a confidence."

"No, no. That's all right. Eugenia simply forgot to mention it to me. She'll no doubt bring it up when she returns."

"Mrs. Quincy is out of town?" George Lehman inquired.

"Yes. She has gone to our summer home on the lake this week. Left yesterday."

Suddenly a dreadful possibility clicked into place in Patterson's mind, and he rose abruptly. Mr. Lehman stood too, looking startled.

"You've done what you can do," Patterson told him. "I'll start someone working to locate the boy immediately. Don't worry. We'll find him." His gaze swept over the director's desk. "We'll get a telephone out here right away. Can't have people running between here and my office when you need me. I'll be in touch with you soon."

Very soon, he thought grimly as he headed for the car, if what he strongly suspected turned out to be fact. Eugenia couldn't have picked up that boy and taken him with her, could she? As he settled into the car behind a silent Gridley, he berated himself for not being more alert.

"Let's go home, Gridley. We have a trip ahead of us this afternoon."

Chapter Eleven

EUGENIA LEARNS A HARD LESSON

On the spacious veranda of the summer house, Eugenia Quincy lay on a chaise lounge and looked out over the lake. On her first day of what was to be a change of scenery, she was tired. She watched Clara and the small boy who walked beside her along the water's edge.

After thinking over the events of yesterday, Eugenia wondered uneasily if she had done the right thing. Very soon after they had reached the open road, Will had fallen asleep on Clara's lap. Eugenia was pleased.

"He's going to be very easy to take care of, Clara," she'd said happily. "I guess children that age sleep a lot. Have you ever had charge of a baby like him?"

"No, mum," the girl had replied. "I was the youngest in my family." She hesitated and then inquired, "What do we feed him?"

Eugenia hadn't considered that. "Why, I suppose whatever we eat. I'm sure Greta has put in enough for all of us. He can't eat a whole lot."

This, she soon discovered, was an understatement. Will wouldn't eat anything. Shortly after their arrival at the lake, Will had awakened. Seeing only strange faces, he started to cry. "Allie. Will wants Allie," he had sobbed.

"What's Allie?" Eugenia asked anxiously. "Is it something to eat? Give him a cookie, Clara."

The cookie was offered, but Will pushed it away. "Ethan? Allie?" He looked around frantically, and huge tears ran down his face.

"For goodness' sake, Clara, give him whatever he wants. We can't have that wailing all afternoon," Eugenia had complained.

"I don't know what he wants," Clara replied, desperation creeping into her voice. "He probably misses his family. Oh, mum! We shouldn't have taken him away from the Home."

"Well, we did, so we'll have to make the best of it. Find something to cheer him up. He's making me nervous."

Clara had done her best, Eugenia was forced to admit, but Will wasn't happy. Throughout the afternoon he continued to

cry, adding "Simon" to his list of grievances. When he had finally
sobbed himself to sleep again, Eugenia was relieved.

"Well, that's over. Do they all do that, Clara?"

"I don't know. But they all need clean clothes, and we don't
have any of those."

"Oh, dear." Eugenia flopped down on the sofa and put her
hand on her forehead. "I'm getting a terrible headache, Clara.
You'll have to take care of it. Go and get some." Without opening her eyes, she waved her hand feebly at the girl. When Clara
didn't move, she sat up in surprise. "Well, what are you waiting
for? You'd better go before he wakes up again. You certainly don't
expect me to do anything with him."

"I never bought a little boy's clothes before. And I got no
way to get to the village. We can't both go unless we take him
with us."

"Oh, bother," Eugenia grumbled. "Why didn't you think of
that before we got here?"

Clara remained silent, as if knowing that whatever she
answered, it was sure to be the wrong thing.

"I suppose I'll have to go. There's probably not a thing in
that village for a child to wear."

Eugenia flung herself out of the house, muttering about
inefficient help, and headed for the little store closest to the lake.
She returned some time later bearing a shirt and short pants.

They were obviously several sizes too large, but she threw them down on the table.

"There. When he wakes up, you can put them on him."

Clara stared at the outfit. "Where's the underwear?"

"Underwear?"

"Yes, mum. He needs more underpants and an undershirt. The ones he's wearing are ... sort of wet."

Eugenia was horrified. "Didn't you take him to the bathroom?"

"He's been asleep. Did you want me to wake him up?"

"No, no. Of course not. He'll start howling again." She sighed irritably. "I'll have to go back. I certainly wish you could think of things like that before I run myself to a frazzle. You don't have anything else to do."

Clara ducked her head. "Yes, mum. I'm sorry, mum."

"You should be. I brought you along to be of some help."

The rest of the afternoon—and the night—hadn't gone any better. Several times Eugenia heard the boy cry. Then she was forced to listen to the creak of the rocking chair until he fell asleep again in Clara's arms.

No wonder Eugenia was so fatigued this morning.

Thankfully, though, aside from a few hiccuping sobs, Will hadn't cried since Clara had gotten him up. But he still refused to eat.

Eugenia moved restlessly on the chaise lounge. This wasn't the way she had pictured her advent into motherhood.

The boy regarded her solemnly, with a small thumb firmly planted in his mouth. Although he had stopped asking for "Allie" or "Ethan," his big eyes held disapproval. It was most disconcerting.

"What else could he possibly want?" she demanded of Clara. "He won't eat, and he's only taken a bit of milk. Don't children eat three meals a day like everyone else?"

"Yes, mum. I think so," Clara replied. Her eyes were heavy with lack of sleep, and she was bouncing Will on her knee in an attempt to entertain him. "Maybe he's homesick. Maybe we should take him back to the Briars."

Eugenia considered this and shook her head. "We can't do that. Mr. Quincy would wonder why we returned so soon." She looked sharply at Clara. "I don't want him to know about this—not yet, at any rate."

"Yes, mum."

"So take the boy down to the lake for a walk. Take a spoon to dig in the sand—or something."

"Yes, mum."

It was going to be a long few days ahead. She couldn't focus her attention on reading or handwork when she had to be concerned about the child.

Eugenia didn't have long to indulge in self-pity. A crunch on the driveway announced the arrival of a familiar limousine, and she sprang to her feet.

The door opened, and Gridley stepped out. "Good afternoon, madam."

"Good afternoon. What—?" she blustered.

Gridley held open the rear door.

Patterson emerged and walked toward the veranda where Eugenia was sitting. "Good day, my dear."

"Patterson! What are you doing here? I thought you were too busy to get away!" Eugenia did her best to hide her dismay.

"I found that I had a short time free. I shall have to return this evening, but I wanted to check and see that all was well here." He ascended the stairs deliberately and sank into a chair beside the chaise lounge. "Lie down again, Eugenia. You look exhausted."

Patterson looked around with seeming indifference. The trees rustled slightly in the breeze, and the lake glistened in the afternoon sun. He watched the water for a moment in silence.

"Isn't that Clara walking along the shore?" he finally asked.

"Why, yes, I believe it is."

"And who does she have with her? It looks like a small boy."

She didn't answer.

"Eugenia?"

She had thought to face him defiantly, but when she raised her eyes to meet his, she crumpled at his stern expression.

"Eugenia, why on earth did you bring that boy up here without letting anyone know you had him? Don't you realize that you could be prosecuted for kidnapping?"

"Kidnapping!" Eugenia was horrified. "I didn't kidnap him! I just borrowed him for a few days. I was going to take him back."

"Didn't you think that the people at the Home would be looking for him 'for a few days'?"

She waved an arm. "Oh, Patterson, he's an orphan. They've got more of those than they need now. And I did ask Mr. Lehman if I might take him—to get acquainted, you know."

"And what did Mr. Lehman say?"

Eugenia tossed her head in disdain. "Oh, he said he thought the boy was too little to be away from people he knew, but I didn't agree with him. The child is too young to know the difference." But even as she said the words, Eugenia recalled the boy's tearstained face and the fact that he hadn't eaten since their arrival.

"Nevertheless," Patterson said, "he must be returned as quickly as possible. The people at the Home, and especially his older brother, are frantic over his disappearance."

"Oh, very well. Send Gridley down to the lake to get him, and you can take him back with you."

"No, Eugenia. I will not take him and make explanations for you. This is your responsibility, and I suggest that you undertake it immediately." He rose and started for the car.

"Patterson!" Eugenia gasped, following him. "I can't do that! What will I say? Besides, I'm quite sure that Mr. Lehman dislikes me."

"Are you, my dear? I wonder why."

Gridley closed the door of the limousine, and Patterson leaned out the window to speak to his wife. "If I were you, I would start at once. I'll see you at dinner."

Eugenia watched as the car turned onto the road leading back to Briarlane. She was furious at Patterson for putting her in this position. She was angry with George Lehman for refusing her permission to take the child when she requested it. If he hadn't been so stubborn, this never would have happened.

She stormed down to the edge of the lawn to summon Clara. If the girl had seen the car, she would know that Eugenia had been ordered home. How humiliating this was!

"Get our things together, Clara," Eugenia snapped. "We're leaving. We'll take the boy back to the orphanage where he belongs." She regarded Will with disfavor. "I can't have him starving to death while he's in my care. I don't understand why you find it so difficult to get food into a two-year-old child." She gestured angrily. "Well, move along! We haven't all day to stand around."

"Yes, mum. If you'll watch the boy, I'll pack the car."

"Put him in the chair on the veranda. I'll see that he doesn't fall out. But hurry. If he starts to cry, you'll have to come and get him."

Dreadful child! Eugenia thought. If they were all like that, she was fortunate not to have any. It would be a relief to get rid of him.

But now another matter called for serious thought. What was she going to say to Mr. Lehman? As soon as the car was packed and they were on the road, Eugenia gave that problem her full attention.

Perhaps she could set Will on the inside of the fence where she had picked him up and go on home. This idea was abandoned almost as soon as it formed. Patterson was sure to demand a full accounting this evening, and she knew what he would say if he discovered that she hadn't faced George Lehman. Patterson was a kind man, but his sense of justice was spread evenly over everyone, including his wife.

As the miles went by, nothing acceptable came to mind. She pictured George Lehman's face if she simply announced that she had taken the boy out of the yard, and her husband made her bring him back. It was unthinkable, but no explanation occurred to her that wouldn't bring the blame squarely down upon her own head.

There was no sound from the backseat. Probably the boy had fallen asleep again. He didn't have to have a story ready to explain his disappearance.

When the car stopped in front of the gate at Briarlane, Eugenia was no closer to a solution than when they had left the lake. Reluctantly she stepped out of the car, removed her driving gloves, and laid them on the seat. Followed by Clara with a sleeping Will in her arms, she began the long trek to the front door of the Briars.

The next few minutes were a blur of activity. The girl who opened the door took in the scene and shrieked, "Will! Here's Will! He's back!" and ran to summon Matron.

The noise brought Mr. Lehman rushing to the hallway. Before Eugenia could open her mouth, he was shaking her hand and smiling broadly.

"Oh, Mrs. Quincy! You've found him! You'll never know how grateful we are to you. His brothers and sister have been so upset—as we all have—and you've brought him back. How can I ever thank you?"

Eugenia leaned against the wall in relief. That was it, of course. She had found the child wandering in the road and had brought him back. Everyone was happy, and that was the end of the matter.

Will had awakened and was crying again. His eager stranglehold on Matron when she took him from Clara's arms brought unexpected tears to Eugenia's eyes.

"Mr. Lehman, I wish to speak with you a moment … if I may," she said.

"Of course." He ushered her into his office and closed the door.

When Eugenia Quincy emerged sometime later from the Briars, she felt drained but calm. For the first time in her life, she had admitted to herself—and to someone else—that she had been wrong. And she had misjudged George Lehman. He had been most understanding and forgiving. Now she would go home and throw herself on the mercy of the court.

Chapter Twelve

HUGH'S DEMAND

Will was the center of attention at supper that evening. Although he allowed the children to hug him, he wouldn't leave the security of Matron's lap. He ate everything offered to him, including an extra pudding.

Matron finally had to call a halt to it. "He's going to be sick all night if you feed him any more." She laughed. "I know we're glad to have him back, but let's save some of the celebration for tomorrow."

"Where'd ya go, Will?" Simon asked him. "How'd ya get out the gate?"

Of course Will couldn't tell him. His only comment was "pretty car."

Bert put the story together quickly. "He went for a ride someplace, that's for sure. And how many cars have you seen around here?"

"Only the big one," Ethan replied. "But Mr. Quincy would've known if he was in that one. I still think he went with Mrs. Quincy. I'm going to watch him from now on, in case she decides to come back."

"We mustn't forget to thank the Lord for bringing Will home safely," Matron said as they prepared for bed that night.

Ethan was surprised. "How do we do that?"

"The same way we asked Him to take care of Will," Matron replied. "We'll thank Him when we pray."

"I guess Matron was right," Ethan confided to Bert later. "It is a good idea to pray about stuff. Do you think the Lord really does have His eye on us every minute?"

Bert nodded. "I heard it in Sunday school, and Matron told us the same thing. She read it in the Bible, so it must be so."

Ethan recalled Ma telling them stories from the Bible. Apparently there were more that he hadn't heard yet. "Doesn't it make you nervous to think of someone watching you all the time?"

"It does if I'm doing something wrong." Bert laughed.

"What happens if you do something wrong, and He sees you?" Bert frowned.

"Well, if I wish I hadn't done it, I say I'm sorry and I won't do it again. Then He forgives me. Matron says the two most important things to say are 'thank you' and 'I'm sorry.'"

Ethan sighed. "God sure has a lot of people to watch. I hope He doesn't miss anyone."

One person at the Home who didn't seem to worry about God watching him was Hugh. He did all he could to make life miserable for the younger children, but no one dared report him to Matron or to Mr. Lehman.

For his part, Ethan kept out of Hugh's way as much as possible. Yet more and more often he found himself finishing Hugh's chores or taking on a disagreeable task when Hugh reminded him of what might happen to boys who knew more than they should.

"How long has Hugh been around here?" Ethan asked Bert. "He acts like he owns the place."

"Just about all his life, I guess," Bert replied. "Him and Riley been here the longest of any." He narrowed his eyes. "You ain't lit into him again, have you?"

"Naw. He can do what he wants to me, but he better not touch my brothers or Alice. What makes him so mean, anyway?"

"He's probably mad 'cause no one adopted him. I remember he had a chance to be farmed out once, but he said if he had to clean another barn, he'd rather stay with this one."

The day before school began, the boys were informed that haircuts would start directly after breakfast. A tall stool was placed in the backyard, and one by one they submitted to the draped towel and the cold scissors wielded by Matron.

"Look at all the extra neck we have to wash," Bert moaned. "And it ain't even the same color as the rest of us. Now Matron can tell if we forgot behind our ears."

He advised Ethan to ignore the snickers and remarks from the girls, but Ethan blushed when Shala pointed out his "rooster tail" and suggested that he put his head under the pump and plaster his hair down.

Nevertheless, he was excited about beginning school. "I won't have to stay home 'cause someone's sick," he confided to Bert. "I can go to school every day."

Unlike Ethan, Hugh became even more sullen as the first day of school approached. "I ain't going back to that school again," he declared to Riley. "I'm big enough to get me a job and earn some money."

"Mr. Lehman won't let you quit school," Riley pointed out. "And you have to live someplace. If you go work on another farm, you might not get any more than you do here—your room and board."

"I ain't going to be no farmer," Hugh replied. "I'm going to be a … a banker!"

"A banker!" Riley hooted. "You, a banker?" Then, seeing the scowl on Hugh's face, he quickly added, "Of course, you're the best one in school in arithmetic. No one else can do problems in his head like you can. Instead of quitting, you should get ready for high school. Then when you graduate, you could get a job in a bank."

Hugh shook his head. "That takes too long. I got to get away now."

"You ain't thinkin' of running away, are you? I wouldn't do that if I were you. You might not ever have it as easy as this again."

"I'll take my chances," Hugh growled.

Riley left him to his thoughts, and Hugh sat watching the younger boys play in the field. When the ball rolled in his direction, he picked it up and held it until Ethan came running after it.

"Here, kid," he said. "You want this back?"

Ethan nodded and held out his hand.

"You gotta pay me for it."

Ethan backed away. "I don't have any money."

"I'm not talking about money. You gotta do something for me."

"What?"

"I'll tell you later. You gonna promise, or do I have to talk to Mr. Lehman?"

"I-I guess so," Ethan stammered. "But what if I can't do it?"

"You can do it all right. You just have to keep your mouth shut. And if I can't trust you …" Hugh left the rest of the threat unsaid.

"You can trust me," Ethan promised. "I haven't said anything yet, have I?"

"And you better not. I'll see you later." Hugh tossed the ball in Ethan's direction and then turned toward the barn.

Ethan ran back to the game, but his heart was no longer in it.

"What's that big bully want now?" Bert inquired. "Do you have to finish his chores?"

"Naw. He didn't say what he wanted. He just talks a lot." Ethan pretended that nothing was wrong, but the big lump in his stomach told him that something dreadful lay ahead.

It wasn't long in coming. Ethan's morning chore was dusting the parlor and hallway and emptying the wastebaskets—the job that had been Bert's the day he met Mrs. Quincy at the door. As Ethan worked, the big front door opened slightly, and Hugh beckoned him out to the steps.

After looking around, Hugh whispered, "I came to tell you what I want you to do. Remember, you promised. You need to do it now."

Ethan was alarmed. "I have to finish my chores, or I'll be in trouble with Matron! I can't leave till she checks."

"You don't even have to stop working," Hugh said. "Have you emptied the trash baskets yet?"

Ethan shook his head. "You want me to empty the ones upstairs, too?"

Hugh looked disgusted. "Naw. Why would I want that? I want you to wait until Mr. Lehman goes out to talk to Otis before you get the wastebasket in the office. Now listen. In the top drawer of Mr. Lehman's desk is a box. It has something in it that … that belongs to me. Just drop the little box in the wastebasket and bring it out to the back with the rest of the stuff. I'll take care of it from there."

"Open Mr. Lehman's desk?" Ethan backed away. "I can't do that! I don't even dust his desk. And he's always there when I empty the trash."

"Keep your voice down! He won't be there today because Otis just sent someone to get him. By the time he gets back, you'll be all through here and gone. Now, you gonna do what I told you or not?"

"I never took anything in my life," Ethan said, "and I'm sure not going to steal from Mr. Lehman. You can do whatever you want to me, but I won't do that."

Hugh looked angry. "Might have known you wouldn't be any good. You can't even keep a promise. I guess we'll have to see if Mr. Lehman believes you never stole nothin' when I tell him about what you took from Riley's cupboard. You'll be sorry!"

Hugh ran down the steps and around the building, and Ethan hurried back into the hallway. He would get the basket from Mr. Lehman's office at once, before Mr. Lehman left. Then the director would know that he hadn't touched anything. But when Ethan reached the office and pushed open the door, Mr. Lehman's chair was empty. He had already left to see Otis.

Now what? Should he risk Matron's disfavor by leaving his job undone, or rush in and get the basket as fast as he could?

To his great relief, Matron spoke from behind him. "Aren't you finished yet, Ethan? What's taking you so long?"

"Mr. Lehman isn't here, and I didn't know if I should go in."

Matron walked in and looked around. "That's odd. He never leaves his office unlocked when he goes out. He must have left in a big hurry." She turned to Ethan and patted his shoulder. "You were right, Ethan. We don't enter the office unless Mr. Lehman is here. Let me get the basket for you. Then I'll lock the door."

She brought out the basket and then turned to push the lock. "No, better not," she muttered. "If he left that fast, he may not have his keys. We'll just close the door and leave it."

Ethan followed Matron to the kitchen. While he was grateful that her arrival saved him from having to make a decision, he was worried about what Hugh would do next. Should he tell Matron what Hugh had asked him to do? No, she might think he had been on his way in when she appeared!

Besides, Ethan didn't trust Hugh not to harm his brothers or Alice. He'd better keep it to himself. When Hugh went to Mr. Lehman, Ethan would have to explain things the best he could and hope that Mr. Lehman would believe him.

Life was hard, Ethan decided. If only he had himself to worry about, it wouldn't be so bad, but he had three others depending on him. He couldn't do anything to get them sent away.

"We ain't got much longer to do this," Bert remarked as he and Ethan fished on the river's edge that afternoon. "You been to school much?"

"Yeah, some," Ethan replied. "I had to stay home to help Ma when she got sick. But I know how to read and write, and I can do some numbers. Will I be in your grade?"

"Probably. You're eight, and so am I. I like school pretty much. 'Course, some of the guys call us 'Thorny,' but I don't pay any attention to that."

"'Thorny'? Why do they call you that?"

"'Cause we're from the Briars," Bert explained. "Some kids from here don't like to be teased, but it doesn't bother me. The town kids found out that you don't call Shala that more than once. She can use her fists as good as any boy. They stay away from her."

Ethan understood that. But before he could open his mouth to say so, someone crashed through the bushes behind them and ran to the river. Almost as though she had heard her name, Shala appeared and plunked herself down beside the surprised boys.

"It's getting kind of crowded in this spot," Bert said in disgust. "Let's go down the river, Ethan."

"Wait," Shala panted. "Wait till I catch my breath. I was sent down to get you."

"What's the matter? Is Will gone again?" Ethan jumped to his feet in alarm.

"Will's fine," Shala assured him. "He's with Matron. Mr. Lehman wants to talk to everyone together, so you have to come back now."

"What's he going to talk about?" Bert asked as they hurried toward the house.

"Don't know," Shala said. "He just said to round everybody up. So I came after you."

"How'd you know where we were?" Bert demanded.

"I saw you start out with your fishing poles." She grinned. "I figured you weren't on the way to the orchard to pick apples."

"Smarty," Bert muttered. "You better not be trying to fool us."

The boys joined the other children in the dining room just before a solemn Mr. Lehman came in.

"Something very serious has happened here today," he said. "A box containing some money belonging to the Home is missing from my desk. I'm not accusing anyone here of taking it. I'm hoping it was misplaced. I only want to ask all of you to keep watch around the house and the barn. If you see any strangers, let one of us know right away."

Mr. Lehman said a few more things, but Ethan wasn't listening. His heart had dropped to his shoes. Could that be the box

Hugh wanted him to get? Did Hugh go back and get it himself after Ethan and Matron had left? If so, he would surely tell Mr. Lehman that Ethan had taken it. Should he try to talk to Hugh about it?

As carefully as he could, Ethan looked around the room for the older boy.

Hugh was nowhere to be seen.

By bedtime everyone knew that Hugh was gone.

"Are we going to ask the Lord to bring him back, like we did Will?" Ethan asked when Matron came to pray with him.

"We'll certainly ask the Lord to protect Hugh and be with him," Matron replied. "I don't reckon he's in as much danger as a little boy would be. He can pretty well take care of himself. But I don't like to see him leave the Home before he finishes school. This is the only family Hugh has ever had."

After Matron had turned out the light and left, Bert asked Riley, "Do you know where Hugh went?"

"Nope."

"Do you think he'll be back?"

"Dunno."

"Did he tell you he was going?"

"Not exactly. He said he didn't want to go back to school. He wanted to get a job and earn some money."

"If they find him, will they bring him back?"

"Maybe, maybe not," Riley answered. "If he got himself apprenticed somewhere, it's likely Mr. Lehman would let him stay. He only had another year to be ready to go out on his own."

Ethan hoped that Hugh wouldn't return. Even though Hugh wasn't in sight, Ethan still worried that he would carry out his threat to go to Mr. Lehman. He knew that Hugh had been angry with him this morning.

Ethan stirred restlessly in his bed. He was the only one who knew that Hugh wanted the box. If only there were someone he could tell about it without getting into trouble. Suddenly his eyes flew open.

If the Lord were watching him every minute, Ethan reasoned, He would be listening, too! Ethan could tell Him. This was a comforting thought. After explaining to the Lord all that had happened that day, Ethan felt much better. He wouldn't tell Mr. Lehman what he knew, Ethan decided. He would let the Lord do that.

Chapter Thirteen

ETHAN MAKES A
SURPRISING DISCOVERY

Hugh didn't appear the next day, either—the first day of school.
As Matron bustled around preparing school clothes for the children, she looked sad.

"I think Matron really misses old Hugh," Ethan remarked.
"I don't see why. I'm glad he's gone."

"So am I," Bert agreed. "But we haven't known him as long
as Matron has. He was younger than Will when he came here."

"How come he grew up to be so ornery? Didn't he want
people to like him?"

"Yeah, prob'ly. But he found out that nobody did when other
kids got adopted and he stayed. Now he's too old for anyone to

want him." Bert chewed thoughtfully on a straw. "I can sorta see how he feels."

Ethan glanced at his friend. "How come you're not ornery?"

Bert grinned. "I like it here. I don't want anybody to adopt me, 'cause my folks might come back. They'd be awful disappointed if I was gone. If they don't show up by the time I'm sixteen, I'll hunt for 'em. How about you? Are you going to look for your pa?"

"I have to stay here until Will is sixteen. I promised Russell I'd look after the little kids."

"Guess you'll never be adopted, then. Not many folks want four at one time."

But Ethan didn't worry about that. He only wanted the Cooper children to stay together.

Later, when the others raced on ahead to the schoolhouse, Ethan held firmly to Alice's hand. The older girls had offered to escort her safely there, but Ethan had declined.

"This is her first day," he'd explained. "I need to make sure she isn't scared or anything. Tomorrow she can go with you."

Alice chatted happily as they walked along.

"Will I get books to take home like the big kids have, Ethan?"

"Yeah, sure. You'll have some books."

"Will I be able to read them tonight?"

Ethan smiled at her. "Not all of them. You may learn some words today, but it takes a while to be able to read a whole book."

Alice sighed. "At least I'll be able to carry them in my book bag." She skipped a little to keep up with Ethan. "I already have a pencil box in there. And a clean hankie that Matron gave me. And an apple for recess."

"Mmm. That's nice." Ethan listened with only half an ear, answering when it seemed appropriate. The others were ahead of them, and he was anxious to get there in time for a game of stickball before classes started. Alice had to run to keep up with him.

"Will you open it for me?" she asked.

"Open what?"

"My pencil box! I just told you!"

"Sure, remind me when we get home this afternoon, and I'll do it."

Alice stopped in the road. "Ethan, I told you it has lots of pencils in it, and I need them for school! You have to do it now."

He could see children running toward the schoolhouse as the bell began to ring.

"I can't, Alice. See? The kids are all going in, and we'll be late if we don't run. Here, let me carry your bag. I'll open the box at recess."

Alice was assigned to the primer class. After an examination, Ethan joined the third reader with Bert. Mr. Smalley welcomed everyone to a new year and started to hand out books. Alice beamed with delight as the primer, speller, and arithmetic book were given to her.

Ethan had already been told that only girls carried book bags. The boys had straps to hold their books together. Even so, he wasn't prepared for the number of books that were handed out.

"… four, five, six, seven! Do we really have to learn all this?" He was astonished and a bit dismayed.

"Yep," Bert replied. "Don't worry about it. Matron helps with studying in the evening. Just pay attention here, and you won't have any trouble."

Ethan wasn't sure about that, but he determined to do his best. For a moment he thought about how proud Ma would be that he was in school. Maybe his older brothers and sister would like to know too. He'd ask Matron to help him write a letter to them.

Lessons were assigned, and everyone settled down to work. When the primer class was called to the front of the room, Ethan looked up to watch Alice walk proudly to the bench beside the teacher's desk. The seat she had been sitting in was directly in front of him, four rows ahead. Ethan glanced at her desk, and his eyes widened in horror.

What was that on her desk? It certainly didn't hold pencils! No wonder Alice couldn't get the box open. It was made of metal and fastened with a lock. As he stared at the box in fascination, Ethan knew exactly what it was and where it had come from, even though he had never seen it.

It was the box of money from Mr. Lehman's desk.

How had Alice gotten it? She couldn't have taken it from the office.

Ethan forgot about the books in front of him. His mind was in a whirl. Somehow he had to get that box and hide it from sight. He started to get up, but Bert tugged on his overall strap.

"You can't walk around without permission," he whispered. "Where ya going?"

Ethan sat back down. There was nothing he could do while the whole room looked on. At recess he'd get the box. By then maybe he'd know what to do with it.

He looked around cautiously to see if anyone else had noticed, but everyone seemed to be reading. Fortunately the older students were in the next room. One of them would certainly recognize the box, and then there would be a lot of explaining to do. The Coopers would be sent away at once.

There was still a lot of explaining to do, Ethan decided as he waited for recess time. Was there any way to get the money box back to the office without anyone knowing?

As soon as the children were dismissed for play, Ethan rushed to the front of the room. "Alice, go get your book bag from the coatroom."

"Why?"

"Because I want to put your … your pencil box in it. We have to take it back home."

"Why?" Alice wailed. "It's mine. Matron said I could keep it. I want the pencils out of it!"

"Don't cry," Ethan said. "Look. I have to take it home to get it open. See? There's nothing here at school to take the lock off. Here, you can have my pencil today. All right?"

Alice was reluctant, but Ethan was finally able to persuade her to give him the box. Quickly he crammed it into the book bag. Now what would he do with it? He couldn't leave the bag in the coatroom, out of sight. What if some other girl took it by mistake or peeked into it at lunchtime?

There was nothing to do but keep it with him. That meant he wouldn't be able to go outside to play all day. Wearily he returned to his desk and put the bag at his feet.

The happy sounds of laughter and games floated in through the open window. Once again, through no fault of his own, Ethan wasn't a part of the fun. If only he had just himself to take care of, life would be a lot easier.

The rest of the morning dragged. Ethan's class hadn't been called on to recite, so he had no reason to leave his seat. At noon, however, he was faced with a dilemma.

"Come on, Ethan. Get your dinner pail and come outside to eat," Bert said.

"Uh, I guess I'll eat in here. You go ahead."

Bert regarded him with suspicion. "What's the matter with you? You never came out for recess. You stuck to that desk or something?"

"Naw," Ethan mumbled. "I think I'll do some extra reading this noon. Tomorrow I'll go out with you." He pulled a book from his desk and flipped it open.

"You gonna read the arithmetic book?" Bert shook his head in disbelief as he made his way to the door.

After looking forward to school all summer, Ethan was disappointed. This certainly wasn't what he had envisioned. As he munched his sandwich, his head ached over the problem of what to do about that pesky box. Any way he looked at it, he could foresee only trouble for the Coopers. What if Mr. Lehman sent him away and made the others stay there?

And where had Alice gotten hold of that box, anyway?

The first class after lunch was penmanship. Ethan sat with his copybook open in front of him and hoped that no one would notice him.

"Ethan?" Mr. Smalley's voice seemed to echo through the room.

"Yes, sir?"

"You're not writing your exercise."

"No, sir."

"I presume you have a good reason for not doing this lesson."

Ethan sank lower into his seat. His face warmed as all eyes turned in his direction. "Yes, sir. I don't have a pencil."

"I see." Mr. Smalley glared at the giggling boys and girls. "And how did you expect to do your work without the proper tools?"

Ethan opened his mouth to answer, but Alice spoke for him. "He gave his pencil to me." Then she added proudly, "He's my brother."

"That's commendable, I'm sure." Mr. Smalley said. "Perhaps you'd let him borrow it this afternoon." He looked at Ethan. "Tomorrow it would be well to provide one for each of you."

"Yes, sir." Ethan bent his head over his copybook.

Would this day never end? At least when school was out, he'd be safe from discovery until he could decide what to do next.

When they were finally dismissed for the day, Ethan strapped his books together and then picked up Alice's book bag. He was determined to hang on to it until they got home.

"You gonna carry her bag every day?" Bert wanted to know. "The guys will tease you for sure."

"She can carry it tomorrow," Ethan answered. "This is her first day. It's pretty heavy for a little girl."

Bert was right. The older boys joined them on the walk home, and they were quick to notice what Ethan had.

"Well, look at mama's boy with the book bag," one of them called. "Maybe we should help him carry it!"

Before Ethan knew what was coming, the boy grabbed the bag and ran with it.

"Hey! Give that back!" Ethan yelled and started after him.

"Here, Fred … catch it!" The boy threw the bag to one of his companions.

In less than a second, the worst happened. The box flew out of the bag, hitting the ground with a thud, and the contents scattered in front of the astonished children.

"Boy, oh boy," Bert muttered as he helped Ethan scoop up the money and stuff it into the book bag. "Are you in for it now!"

A silent group of children gathered as Ethan and Bert continued to pick up the money and put it in Alice's book bag. No one offered to help them, even though some of the bills had blown over into the grass beside the road.

"I hope we got it all," Bert finally said when they thought they'd picked up the last piece. "Do you know how much was in there?"

Ethan shook his head. "I never saw it before."

Bert looked him in the eye. "I know you never took it. And we know that Alice didn't. So how did it get there?"

Ethan had no answer. He could think only about what needed to be done. He closed the bag securely and then grabbed Alice's hand. After the first cry when the boy had snatched the book bag, she too had remained silent. Now she hurried along between Ethan and Bert.

"There weren't any pencils in my box, were there, Ethan?" Tears rolled down her cheeks. "The teacher said we both had to have one by tomorrow. What will we do?"

"You'll have a pencil, Alice. Don't worry." *I'm sure I won't be needing mine,* he thought glumly.

Bert sighed. "The first day of school is usually hard, but I never seen anything like this before. It makes my stomach hurt to think about it. Where did you get that box anyway?"

"I don't know," Ethan answered, sounding miserable. "It was in Alice's bag. She said she had a pencil box, and I never saw it until we were in school."

Alice sniffed again. "Matron told me I could keep it."

"Did Matron see the box, Alice?" Bert asked her.

"No. I put it away for school."

"But who gave it to you?"

"Nobody. I found it out by the barn. Otis said he didn't want it." Alice bit her lip. "Are we in trouble, Ethan?"

"You're not," he replied. "We'll just hope that Mr. Lehman doesn't think I'm the one who left it out there."

"So what are you going to do?" Bert inquired. "Are you going right to his office as soon as we get home?"

Ethan looked sick. "I suppose I'll have to. Nearly every kid in school knows about it. What do you think he'll do?"

Bert shrugged. "Don't know. Nothing like this has ever happened since I've been here. But I never saw Mr. Lehman whip anyone, even when they did something real bad."

"He could send me away."

Bert didn't reply.

Matron met the children at the front door of the Briars. "Put your books away and change your clothes, boys," she said. "Otis needs you in the barn for a job. Then you can play until suppertime. We'll work on your lessons right after you eat."

Ethan pushed the book bag into the cupboard and was grateful for some extra time before he had to face Mr. Lehman. He couldn't understand, however, why none of the other children were rushing to tell what they'd seen. Several of the onlookers had been from the Home, including Shala.

Ethan mentioned this to Bert, who seemed surprised at the question.

"Nobody tells nothin' to Mr. Lehman," Bert explained. "You're expected to take care of stuff yourself. We don't tell on anyone around here."

"You mean if I never told Mr. Lehman about the money, he wouldn't ever know?"

"Prob'ly not. But the other kids would know, and they prob'ly wouldn't play with you or nothin'."

Ethan thought this over as he did his chores. That meant that Hugh was bluffing him when he threatened to go to the director. Did it also mean that he couldn't tell what he knew about Hugh? *Of course it did*, he thought. He wouldn't be able to tell Mr. Lehman that Hugh had asked him to get the box from the drawer, and that he had refused.

Ethan decided there was nothing else to do except take the blame for the whole thing. He couldn't say that Alice found the box. She was too little to be responsible. Besides, it wasn't her fault. It was his for not standing up to Hugh. Whatever punishment was coming belonged to him.

Chapter Fourteen

GRIDLEY PICKS UP
A STRANGER

Gridley, the Quincys' driver, stood beside the big touring car and
scanned the deserted road. This was a most annoying circum-
stance. If he hadn't taken his eye from the road when a rabbit
ran out of the bush, he could have avoided the rock that lay in
the center of his path. He winced, remembering the grinding
sound of a hole being torn in the crankcase oil pan. By the time
he stopped the car, all the oil had run out and soaked into the
dusty road.

He could make an emergency repair, but unfortunately he
had neglected to bring a supply of oil. The nearest village was
only a mile or so down the road, but it might as well have been

ten or twenty miles, for Gridley dared not leave the car to go get it.

He glanced at the sun and then took a watch from his pocket. He should have reached the summer house by now, where Mr. and Mrs. Quincy awaited the car to bring them home.

Gridley prided himself on the care of his automobiles. How could he have been so thoughtless as to start out without extra oil? Well, he had, and the chances of anyone coming along this back road to rescue him were slim indeed.

He sat on the running board and pondered his alternatives. He had already rejected the thought of abandoning the car. That left waiting for another conveyance or a passerby who would be willing to help him.

The late afternoon was cool, and the view from where he sat was pleasant, but Gridley was in no mood to enjoy it. When half an hour passed with no change in the scenery, he started to pace.

Suddenly, across the field, a man appeared. His head was bent, and he apparently hadn't seen the car in the road. Gridley watched his approach. He was carrying a knapsack and seemed to be in no hurry. Gridley was about to call to him when the fellow looked up, stopped, and then turned as if to go back the way he had come.

Gridley waved his arms frantically. "Hello! Hello, there! Can you help me?"

The figure hesitated and then walked slowly toward the road. As he came nearer, Gridley saw it wasn't a man but a boy.

"I'm having some trouble here," Gridley said. "If you could go up to the next village and get some oil for the car, I'd make it worth your while."

The boy gazed with admiration at the shiny vehicle and rubbed his hand lovingly over the hood. "Sure, mister. I'll go."

Gridley handed him a bill. "This should do it. I need four quarts of oil. By the way, what's your name?"

"Hugh. Hugh Kelly."

"You live around here?"

"Well, I'm sort of traveling right now."

Gridley studied the boy. *Fifteen, maybe sixteen*, he figured. *Old enough to look out for himself.* "All right. You can leave your knapsack here if you like. I'll watch it."

"It's not heavy. I'll take it with me." Hugh trotted off toward the village.

Gridley sat down and watched as the boy disappeared around a bend in the road. *That may be the last I'll see of him or the money*, he thought. *But it's the only chance I've had so far to get out of here.* He leaned against the car and prepared to wait.

Within the hour, Gridley was relieved to see the boy returning.

Hugh handed over the cans of oil and dug in his pocket for the change.

"You can keep that for your trouble," Gridley told him.

When Hugh's face lit up, Gridley decided the boy hadn't been in possession of much money in the past.

Gridley poured the oil into the car and then shined the already immaculate engine. "I'm on my way up to Scott Lake. Can I drop you somewhere?"

Hugh grinned with delight. "I was going that way myself. I'd be glad to keep you company."

Hugh looked around with pleasure as the car purred along the road. They must have been going at least twenty miles an hour, he figured. He'd never ridden that fast in his life.

Wait until I tell the fellows about this! he thought. Then he remembered—he had no intention of returning to the Home. He was on his own.

"So, are you finished with school, Hugh?"

"Yes, sir. I'm through." He looked over at Gridley. The man appeared friendly enough. Hugh might as well tell him the truth. "Actually I got another year to go, but I figure I can do better with my life than sitting in a schoolhouse every day."

Gridley nodded. "Do you have a job waiting up this way?"

"Not exactly," Hugh admitted, "but I'm sure I can find one. I'm a good worker. What I need is a place where there aren't a lot of little kids hanging around all the time."

"Oh. Come from a big family, I guess?"

"Uh, yeah. I suppose you could say that."

Gridley was pretty sure he knew just how large a "family" Hugh came from. Hugh wasn't the first runaway the Briars had known.

"My boss hires young men to work at the courthouse," Gridley said. "They work as messengers and train to be clerks. I could speak to him about a place for you if you'd like."

Hugh turned to him with a look of disbelief. "You could? You mean you really would?"

"You need to realize that he's a strict boss. You'd have to toe the mark and obey orders."

Hugh nodded, grinning.

"It would mean you'd have to go back to town, you know. So if you find something up here you'd like more, you'd better take it."

Hugh said nothing, but Gridley noted the disappointment on the boy's face. Obviously he had run away from the Home and was reluctant to return.

After that, the conversation turned to other matters, and in half an hour, they approached the lake and the summer home.

Mr. Quincy met them in the driveway. "Well, Gridley. Have some trouble along the way, did you?"

"Yes, sir. I hit a rock in the road and had to repair the oil pan. This young fellow was good enough to get more oil for me."

"That so? Well, we appreciate that. Both of you go right to the kitchen. Clara has kept your supper hot. We won't try to go back tonight. We'll leave first thing in the morning. You can find a bed back there for the young man."

"Yes, sir." Gridley motioned for Hugh to follow him and started around the house.

Mr. Quincy stopped the boy. "What's your name, son?"

"Hugh. Hugh Kelly, sir."

"Kelly. Kelly. Haven't I seen you before?"

"No, sir. I don't think so."

"There's a boy at the Briars with that name," Mr. Quincy said. "He'd be about your age. You're not that one, are you? No, no. He wouldn't be that far away from home. Go along and eat your supper."

Hugh breathed a sigh of relief as he followed Gridley to the kitchen.

"You can take a walk down by the lake," Gridley told him when they had finished eating. "Clara will fix your bed. We'll turn in early tonight."

Hugh nodded and then headed for the lake, still carrying his knapsack.

"Don't know what that kid has in the sack, but he won't let loose of it," Gridley said to Clara. "Likely everything he owns. He was honest enough not to run off with my money, so I doubt he's carrying anything that doesn't belong to him."

Hugh sat by the water and skipped a few stones across the surface. He couldn't believe his good fortune. Not only had he ridden in the grandest car he'd ever seen, but the possibility of a job had been offered to him. He'd never go back to that orphanage again. And tonight he wouldn't sleep in a field, as he had last night.

As darkness fell, Hugh got up and started back to the house. He had never seen such a fancy place before. Lights shone through the open windows, and he could see Mr. Quincy sitting at a desk.

But then Hugh's heart seemed to stop beating, for he could hear very clearly what the man was saying.

"Mr. Lehman? Patterson Quincy here. Glad we got that telephone in for you. No, I'm not at home. I'm here at the summer place ... You say you've been trying to get me? Something wrong, is there?... Yes, I see ... Any idea how much was in there?… I suppose you have no idea who could have taken it?… No, of course you don't want to think he'd take it, but listen, George. Here's a coincidence for you. The boy has turned up here. My driver picked him up on the road … Yes, yes. We're coming back in the morning … I'll wait until we get there to talk to him … Yes. We'll meet in your office … I'm sure we'll straighten this out. Maybe it will turn up before then … Yes, see you tomorrow."

Hugh turned away from the window in a panic. What could he do?

Before he could reach a decision, Gridley rounded the corner and spied him. "There you are, Hugh. I was just going down to the lake to get you. Clara has your bed ready. If you've been on the road since morning, you'll probably be glad for some sleep, eh?"

"Yes, sir." Hugh walked with Gridley to the small room at the back of the house. He closed the door and perched on the edge of the bed to think.

In the living room, Patterson Quincy had finished his conversation with George Lehman and sat in thought as well.

"You were going to tell Mr. Lehman about the offer you've had," his wife said. "I didn't hear you mention it."

"Something else came up, Eugenia," Patterson replied. "I'll need to visit his office in the morning. We'll discuss it then. Probably better than trying to explain it over the telephone."

Eugenia dropped her embroidery in her lap. "Do you really feel that this plan is a good one, Patterson? Will it be the best thing for these children?"

"I've heard that it has been most successful in New York City and Chicago. The agents check the homes very carefully before the children are placed in them. The program has been working well for many years now, and we have sufficient time to check it out thoroughly before the next group is assembled."

"But a train? I just can't see those little children put on a train and sent way out west by themselves. They'll be frightened to death!"

"They won't be alone, Eugenia," her husband reassured her. "They'll be escorted the whole way. And it's not as though no one will be expecting them. I understand the advertising is most efficient. It will be the only chance some of these children will ever have to belong to a family."

"You're probably right," Eugenia said. "How many will be taken from the Briars?"

"At least ten. We should begin at once to check the records and choose the most eligible."

"I hope the Cooper children will be among them," Eugenia said. "Is that possible?"

"If we locate the father, or failing that, get permission from the older brother, I would say so. There could be some difficulty in placing four children in one home, but some prosperous farmer might be persuaded to take all of them. They will certainly be considered when we make our decision."

Patterson tilted his head toward his wife. Eugenia seemed to have grown older—well, maybe not older but more thoughtful. There was a notable difference in her since the incident with the Cooper child.

He recalled the day. Dinner that evening had been a silent affair.

"Well, my dear, I presume your interview with Mr. Lehman was satisfactory?" he'd said finally.

"Yes. He was most understanding. Patterson, you were right when you suggested that I wasn't ready for the responsibility of a child. My reasons for wanting the little boy were selfish ones. I thought of him more as a plaything rather than a son. It would have been a mistake to keep him."

Patterson had been so surprised at this confession that the lecture he had intended to deliver was forgotten. This was a side of Eugenia he had never seen before. From that day on, she had been less demanding and seemed more contented with her home.

Ethan wasn't hungry for supper. His stomach hurt, and he pushed the food around his plate.

"You gotta eat your supper, or Matron'll think you're sick," Bert whispered to him. "Shove it in whether you want it or not. Can I have your cake?"

Ethan nodded and did his best to clear his plate. The hour after mealtime was spent on lessons. Baths and bed followed, and Ethan found Matron praying with him and telling him good night before he'd had a chance to take care of his problem.

Even though he was tired, Ethan's eyes wouldn't close. He lay still and stared at the ceiling until he was sure the others were asleep. Then, as quietly as possible, he crept from his bed and took the box from his cupboard.

He tiptoed down the long stairway and into the darkened hall. The office door was open. Ethan could see the light. But when he reached the room and peeked in, he heard Mr. Lehman talking on the telephone.

"The box just disappeared from my desk," he was saying. "No, I don't … I don't want to suspect any of my children, but—"

Ethan heard no more, for he turned and raced back to the bedroom. His heart beat wildly as he returned the box to his cupboard and went back to bed. Was Mr. Lehman talking to the police? Ethan wondered if they would put him in jail. If they found the box while he was in school tomorrow, would they come and get him? Ethan curled up in bed and tried to think of what he must do.

Chapter Fifteen

ETHAN TELLS HIS STORY

The next morning at the appointed time, Mr. and Mrs. Quincy walked out to the touring car for the ride back to town. Clara had already taken her place in front.

Mr. Quincy looked around. "Where's the young boy, Gridley? Does he know it's time to leave?"

"I don't know, sir. He wasn't in his bed when I went to wake him this morning."

~

Ethan must have looked ill, for Matron put her hand on his forehead. "Are you coming down with something, Ethan? We'd better go upstairs and take your temperature."

Once they were upstairs, Ethan sat on the side of his bed, and Matron watched him with concern. "I think you'd better stay home today. I'll tell Mr. Lehman …"

She didn't finish her sentence, for suddenly Ethan threw himself into her lap and burst into tears. Matron smoothed his hair and patted his back until his sobs ended. "Now, now," she said, "suppose you tell me all about it. What is so bad that it's made you sick? You didn't have trouble at school, did you?"

Ethan gulped. "I don't want to be sent away from here."

"Now, why would you worry about that? Nobody is going to send you away."

Suddenly it was impossible to keep it to himself any longer. Ethan told Matron the whole story, beginning with finding Riley's picture on the floor and seeing Hugh in the bedroom, and ending with all that had happened yesterday.

Matron listened without interrupting and then hugged Ethan tightly. "You should have told Mr. Lehman or me all of this at once, but I know you were afraid. You've had a lot to worry you since you've been here. Come, we'll talk to Mr. Lehman now. I'll go with you."

Ethan took the box from his cupboard, and Matron tucked it under her arm. She took Ethan's hand in hers, and together they walked down to the office.

Mr. Lehman wasn't alone. Mr. Quincy was there, and the two men looked very serious.

"We had no idea he would leave before daybreak," Mr. Quincy was saying. "He seemed like a nice young boy. Gridley thought he had real possibilities."

Matron knocked softly on the open door, and Mr. Lehman stood.

"Come in, Matron. Is something wrong? Is Ethan sick?"

"No, I don't think so. But he has something to tell you." She placed the metal box on the desk in front of the two men.

"Why … where did this come from? Ethan, you didn't—"

"No, Mr. Lehman," Matron interrupted. "He didn't take it. You'd better hear the whole story."

Ethan was more frightened than he had ever been in his life, but he managed to tell the director and Mr. Quincy all he had told Matron earlier.

When he had finished, Mr. Lehman asked, "Did you see Hugh after he asked you to get the box?"

"No, sir," Ethan replied. "Bert and I went fishing, and Hugh was gone when we got back."

"On the morning you saw Hugh in the bedroom, did he take anything?"

"I didn't see him take anything. He just opened and shut the cupboards."

"All right, Ethan. I'm glad you've told us this and brought the money back. You may go on to school now. Matron will write a note to the teacher so you won't be marked tardy."

Patterson Quincy waited until the door of George Lehman's office closed behind Matron and Ethan. Then he said, "We don't have all the pieces of the puzzle yet. If Hugh didn't take the box, who did? And if he did take it, why was it found out by the barn? Had the boy been at the Briars long?"

"He came as an infant," Mr. Lehman replied. "He was brought in by a mission worker who had no idea who his parents were. We've never had any request for information about him. Until a few years ago, he was a happy, cheerful boy. He was disappointed when others were adopted and he wasn't, but there were always boys his age to play with, and Hugh seemed to accept the situation."

"What happened, then?" Patterson inquired.

"When he was about twelve, his special friend, Paul, was adopted by a couple who lived several hundred miles from here. Hugh began to change after that. He wasn't openly defiant, but he started to tease the younger children and, I'm sorry to say, bullied them into doing what he wanted them to do. I don't believe he ever actually stole anything, but he would hide things and suggest that someone else might have taken them. The older fellows, like Riley and Philip, were onto his tricks, but the younger boys were afraid of him."

Mr. Lehman leaned back in his chair and sighed. "I talked with him many times about his behavior, and he always promised to do better. But this is the first time he's ever run away. This will be his last year of school, and Hugh is a bright boy. He could have apprenticed in almost any trade he chose if he didn't want to continue his studies."

Patterson listened quietly to the story. "I think we should find the boy. I'd like to see him make something of himself."

A sound in the hallway caused both men to look toward the door. There, with his knapsack in his hand and looking very tired, stood Hugh.

Chapter Sixteen

HUGH MAKES THINGS RIGHT

When the children returned from school in the afternoon, it didn't take long for the news to spread that Hugh had come home.

"He can do whatever he wants to me," Ethan told Bert, "as long as he leaves Alice and the boys alone. Riley'll be glad to have him back. Matron will too."

Bert nodded. "What'll you do when he finds out you told Mr. Lehman about him?"

"I don't know. You're the only one who knows that, besides Matron. I had to tell them something when I came home with all that money. Do you think I should have said I didn't know anything about it?" Ethan was really worried.

Bert considered this. "Naw. It's always best to tell the truth. That way you don't have to keep making up stuff to go with it. But I don't know if Hugh's going to think so."

Ethan was sitting on the back steps when Hugh came out the door.

"Move over, kid," Hugh said.

Ethan moved, and Hugh sat down beside him.

"I hear you had a ride in Mr. Quincy's big car."

Ethan nodded.

"Mr. Gridley told me. Some car, eh?"

Ethan nodded again. He couldn't think of anything to say, since he had no idea where the conversation was going. He waited for Hugh to continue.

"Say, listen, kid. Mr. Lehman said he asked you if you ever saw me take anything, and you said you didn't. How come you never told him I took the box out of his drawer?"

"I didn't know that," Ethan replied. "I just knew that it was gone and you were gone."

"I took it," Hugh admitted. "But I never went away with it. I left it out by the barn."

Ethan looked directly at Hugh. "Yeah. Alice found it there. I had to take it back to Mr. Lehman."

"I know. It wasn't your fault. Look"—Hugh sighed—"I was mean to you because I was scared you'd talk. I wasn't really going to tell on you."

"I know. Bert told me they don't do that here. But I didn't know that, and I was scared too. I was afraid Mr. Lehman would send me away."

"He wouldn't do that. The only reason you leave here is if you get adopted. I'm too old for that now, but you might have a chance someday. You're a pretty good kid."

Ethan was pleased. This was the same as Hugh saying he was sorry. Ethan was willing to forget the past and be friends.

"You going back to school, Hugh?"

"Yeah … I think I will. Gridley says Mr. Quincy might even give me a job if I work hard. I got to start taking care of myself soon." Hugh stood and gave Ethan a friendly poke on the shoulder. "See you later, kid."

He sauntered off toward the barn, leaving Ethan to think that his world had turned upright again. Simon and Will were safe during the day, and Alice was in school with him. He had nothing to worry about.

Even so, Ethan's heart skipped a beat when Matron told him after supper that Mr. Lehman wanted to see him in his office.

"You don't have to be scared if you didn't do nothin' wrong," Bert assured him. "He prob'ly just wants to tell you something."

Mr. Lehman smiled at Ethan when he entered the office. "I've heard from your older brother, and he sent you a letter."

"From Russell? Does he want us to come home?"

"I'm afraid it's not that. I'm sure he'll tell you in here." He handed an envelope to Ethan.

"Thank you. Can I read it now?"

"Certainly. Sit there on the sofa if you like."

Ethan turned the letter over in his hand several times before he opened it and pulled out a single sheet of paper.

Dear Ethan,

I hope you and the others are well. I am writing to tell you that Pa has decided not to come back from the merchant marines. He says we can do whatever we want about staying here. Rachel is going to marry John Higgins, and Walter and Jake and I are working on farms. Mrs. Kenny is going to keep Molly, so we're leaving this house.

I wrote to Mr. Lehman and told him that you could be adopted now. You'll have a nice family to live with and maybe get to finish school. Don't forget that all of you have to stay together. Ma wanted it that way. Rachel and the others send their love.

Your brother,
Russell

Ethan put the letter down. "So they don't want us anymore," he murmured.

Mr. Lehman came around the desk and sat beside Ethan on the sofa. He put his arm around the boy. "I'm sure they would take you if they could. But they have no home together now. It was good of Russell to make arrangements for your future care. I believe he's done the best he could do. I think he's right that some good family may want you."

"All of us," Ethan reminded him. "We all have to go with the same family."

Mr. Lehman agreed. "We'll be sure of that. You won't be separated."

Ethan returned to his room, and Matron comforted Ethan when they prayed together at bedtime. "Don't forget that the Good Shepherd is watching over all of you. He'll never allow you to go anyplace that He doesn't go with you. You're His child, Ethan, and He loves you."

Better than my pa, Ethan thought as he closed his eyes. *At least the Lord keeps His eye on us. I'm glad Matron told me about Him.*

Patterson Quincy sat on the broad porch of his home that evening and looked out over the lawn and garden. The evening paper was on the table beside him, and several matters he hadn't attended to during the day awaited his attention. But he couldn't think about any of those things. Instead he replayed the scene in the office of the Briarlane Children's Home that morning.

Although he had been president of the board of trustees at the Briars for a number of years, Patterson hadn't taken a personal interest in anything other than the business affairs of the institution. He had faithfully watched over the legal matters of the Home and carefully monitored the way the orphanage was run. Although he viewed the children at the Briars as individuals with different needs and personalities, that fact hadn't made a personal impact on him until today.

His mind returned to the scene from this morning. He had observed two badly frightened boys awaiting judgment. That wasn't an unusual experience for Patterson. He faced the guilty and the innocent daily in his courtroom and impartially dispensed justice to the best of his ability. Why then could he not regard these young boys as just two more in a long line of defendants? Perhaps it was because, as he listened to Hugh Kelly, Patterson understood the feelings of rejection the boy expressed, and his attempts to take control of a situation that was not of his own making.

While Patterson hadn't been a homeless child, he had been raised by a couple who didn't encourage him to better himself. They had cared for his needs and expected him to plow a few acres of land for the rest of his life, but Patterson had seen more and had fought for it.

So had Hugh, he thought, as he heard the boy's story.

"When Ethan wouldn't get the money for me," Hugh said, "I thought I'd have to make one of the older boys do it. But Matron didn't lock the office door, so I took it myself. I was going to go as far away as I possibly could, and maybe get a job working in a bank."

"But you didn't take the money with you. Why not?" Mr. Lehman had asked him.

"I got to thinking that the folks here have been awful good to me. And I'm strong. I can earn my own money. So I brought it back and left it by the barn where Otis would find it."

"Why did you decide to come back today, Hugh? You could have gone on and gotten a job."

"I heard Mr. Quincy talking to you last night," Hugh had replied. "I knew you hadn't found the box. Mr. Gridley trusted me with his money, and that felt good. So I decided to come back and take my punishment. I want you to trust me."

The boy was frightened, and Patterson's heart had gone out to him. Hugh was a fighter, and he needed someone to back him up.

The rest of the day Patterson had thought of Hugh Kelly. He was no longer a name on the roster of the orphanage, but a boy who deserved to have someone take an interest in him and make a difference. Patterson Quincy was that someone.

To his astonishment, Patterson found himself thinking that he would like to adopt Hugh. Unlike Eugenia, who now seemed satisfied to remain childless, Patterson wished for a son to carry on his name, and perhaps even follow in his footsteps. Now here was a boy who had many of the same ambitions Patterson had himself as he grew up. This was a boy he'd like to take into his family.

But how would Eugenia feel about it? If there were the least reluctance on her part, Patterson decided, he would abandon the plan immediately. Her happiness was more important to him.

"Eugenia," he began, "I must tell you what occurred today."

Patterson repeated the story and then concluded, "I've been thinking that I would like to apprentice Hugh. I would encourage him to finish school, and then help him get training in the profession he chooses to follow. I'm sure George Lehman would arrange for him to stay at the Briars until he could manage on his own. What do you think?"

Eugenia was silent for so long that Patterson decided she must want nothing to do with the idea. Finally she said, "I wouldn't want the boy to remain at the orphanage, Patterson. We have more than enough room here. You'll want to watch his progress, and it seems to me that he would benefit from your

experience. A child needs a home and a family, don't you think?"
Eugenia returned to her handwork, adding, "Perhaps you would
want to give him our name, if that pleases you. There is something very sad about a boy who reaches the age of fifteen without
a name that attaches him to somebody. I think your plan is an
excellent one."

Chapter Seventeen

A STRANGER VISITS BRIARLANE

Ethan turned nine in November. He decided he really enjoyed school. "I might even be a teacher so I can go to school for the rest of my life," he confided to Bert.

"What about being a farmer?" Bert inquired. "You said that's what you would like the best."

"I'll do that too. I can farm before school and after school and on Saturdays."

Bert said he wasn't sure that was a good idea. It sounded like a lot of work to him. "There's more to farming than hoeing the garden and feeding the animals," he reminded Ethan. "Are you going to stay here at the Briars the rest of your life too?"

Ethan surveyed the big orphanage, the barn, and the surrounding fields. "I wouldn't mind. Since we don't have anyplace to go back to, this is home. I have a lot of years until Will grows up anyway. I can't do anything else until then."

Toward the end of winter, Bert spotted a visitor who was a stranger to the Briars. This was an unusual occurrence, and Bert was quick to report it to Ethan.

"Did you see the man who came to see Mr. Lehman?" Bert said. "He came from the city."

"How can you tell?" Ethan demanded. "He might have come right from Briarlane."

"Nope. I've seen all the people in this town who dress up fancy like that, and he's not one of them. Besides, I heard him ask Otis who the director was here and how to find him. Everyone from town would already know that."

The boys peered toward the house from their perch on the front fence.

"He's staying in there an awful long time," Ethan noted. "I wonder if he'll take someone away with him."

"Not likely. Fathers and mothers come together to choose a kid. This is something else."

When the stranger stayed for dinner, the matter took on a new seriousness. The dining room was quiet, and everyone was on their best behavior as they waited to find out what the visit might mean.

Mr. Lehman looked around and smiled. "These aren't the ordinary sounds of mealtime here," he assured the man. "We so seldom have a guest that the children aren't sure what they ought to do. But this does give you the best chance to see them all together."

"This is a nice group of children," the visitor said. "You'll have difficulty deciding which ones will benefit most from our program. We'll begin to advertise in local newspapers at once for the group that will leave in the spring. I suggest that you have your list ready by the end of April, so your children can leave after school is out."

Mr. Lehman nodded. "I'll have twelve names for you by that time. There will probably be four or five girls in that number. We always have more boys, it seems."

The visitor scanned the strong, healthy-looking children with approval. "We'll have no difficulty placing your children, I'm sure. It might be well to mention this plan in your next letter to your supporters. Some may come forward with a request."

Mr. Lehman thought for a moment. "Several years ago we placed a sister and her little brother with a couple who live in the west," he said. "They may be willing to take another child. Our letter goes to many churches out there, so the word will spread quickly."

The visitor seemed pleased to hear this. "One of our agents and a nurse of your choice will travel with the children. The agent is your link between the Briars and the family who takes a child. He will check the references in each town and act on your behalf. If there are brothers and sisters in your group, we do all we can to place them in the same or nearby communities."

"I have a family of four, ages three to nine," Mr. Lehman told him. "They must go to the same home."

"The same home! I can't recall anyone ever taking four children at once. Are you sure they can't just be settled close to each other?"

Mr. Lehman shook his head. "It is the expressed wish of the family, and I have agreed to abide by it. There is very little say that these children have over their lives, and I feel I must honor my commitment."

"I understand," the man replied. "It would certainly help if we had a request for that many, but we'll do our best."

"I believe the Lord will provide a home for the Coopers," Mr. Lehman said. "If this is His purpose for them, it will surely be done."

The visitor agreed, and after discussing with Mr. Lehman other matters concerning the program, he left.

That week Mr. Lehman sent out a letter to friends and supporters of the Home, explaining the plan to be carried out.

Twelve children from the Briarlane Christian Children's Home will be chosen to travel to the western states on the Orphan Train. In each community where the train stops, people will be asked to take a child into their home and raise him or her as a member of their family. The child will receive an adequate education, religious training, board and room, and the care and consideration a natural child would expect from his or her parents. I would urge each of you to consider the possibility of welcoming one of these children into your home.

Included in Briarlane's twelve will be a family of four children— three boys and a girl. This is the largest number from one family to be offered for adoption in the history of the Home. Since they must be kept together, I am asking that you help us by making inquiry in your church and among your neighbors about a family willing to accept these children.

Please watch your local newspaper for the dates that the Orphan Train will arrive in your community.

Very shortly after this announcement was sent, the children at the Home were told of the upcoming event. There was great excitement as they listened to Mr. Lehman explain the plan. Most of them had seen the train that came through Briarlane on the trip between New York and Chicago, but no one had ever ridden on one.

"You mean we get to ride to Chicago, and someone will take us home with them?" Philip asked.

"That's right," Mr. Lehman assured him. "But you'll have to go past Chicago. Another train will take you farther west." He held up a large map of the United States. "The Orphan Train will go through Missouri, Iowa, Nebraska, and Kansas."

There was silence as the boys and girls took this in. It was hard to believe that such a thing could be possible.

"How many of us will get to go, Mr. Lehman?" was the most common question.

"Twelve of you will leave when school is out," he replied. "More will be ready to go at the end of the summer."

Bert looked troubled. "What if our folks come for us after we're gone?"

"If that should happen, I will know exactly where you are and will let you know at once. No one will be sent on the train from Briarlane unless he or she really wants to go," Mr. Lehman assured them.

Riley was excited about the trip. "I never thought I'd get adopted, seeing as I'm so old. Are you sure they want big fellows like me?"

"Perfectly sure, Riley. You'll be apprenticed, and when you're seventeen, you may stay there and earn wages, or you may go out on your own, just as you would if you remained here. The nice thing will be a family of your own."

"Maybe we won't like our family," someone ventured.

"Then you won't have to stay," Mr. Lehman said. "I won't leave you in a home where you're unhappy. You'll be given another place, or you may come back here."

The children couldn't imagine not being happy in a real home with real parents, but some of them did have fears about leaving Briarlane.

"What will we do without Matron?" Betsy asked.

"Matron will be traveling with you," Mr. Lehman told her. "She will stay with you until you are in your new homes. Then you'll have a mama and papa to look after you. Not all orphans are fortunate enough to have a new life offered to them. Some of you have waited a long time to be adopted, and I'm happy to see you get this chance."

As they talked this over among themselves, most everyone agreed that it would be a great adventure. The little ones who weren't yet in school knew that something unusual was going to happen, but they weren't old enough to remember what a family was like, if they had ever been a part of one. The older boys and girls looked forward to having the things they'd only dreamed about—a mother and father, possibly even brothers and sisters of their own.

But not everyone was anxious to go. When Ethan spoke to Hugh about it, the older boy expressed his view.

"If I have a chance to work for Mr. Quincy, I'd rather stay here." Hugh seemed thoughtful as he looked out across the field. "Mr. Quincy likes me, you know. There aren't a whole lot of folks who do. He thinks I can make something of myself, and when I do, I want to be here, where he can see it. How about you? Does it sound like a good idea to you?"

Ethan poked in the dirt with a stick. "I'd like it. But I think Bert is right. Nobody's going to choose a boy who has so much to take care of. And I won't go without them," he said fiercely. "The boys are still little, and Alice is a girl. Ma wanted me to be in charge."

Hugh had no answer to that.

Chapter Eighteen

THE COOPER CHILDREN
BEGIN A NEW ADVENTURE

As March ended and the time came closer for final arrangements to be made for the Orphan Train, George Lehman was concerned about the fate of the Cooper children. This would be a wonderful opportunity for them, but he dared not send them out unless a definite offer had been made to care for them.

"I would rather that all our children had assigned homes," he told his wife. "I'd like to check each family personally before they take a child. I know that isn't possible, of course, but I'd feel better about it."

"Yes, so would I. I keep thinking how some will feel if their friends are chosen and they are left to go on to the next town."

Mr. Lehman agreed. "It's not a perfect plan, but I don't feel that I should deprive any child of a chance for a home and a good future. We must do the best we can and trust God to look after their welfare. This may well be the only opportunity some of them have."

The time finally came in April when the director was forced to make a decision about the twelve who would be sent out on the first train. Reluctantly he made plans to choose four other children for this trip and hoped that the Coopers might be included in the summer group.

"We have to pray about this," Bert said to his friend. "Matron says that the Bible tells us not to worry about things, but to pray and let the Lord know what we want. Have you been doing that?"

Ethan assured him that he had. "I'm not going to worry until school is out and it's time to go," he said. "Then I might worry a little."

Then a letter arrived that cheered Mr. Lehman and caused great rejoicing among the boys.

Willow Creek, Nebraska
10 April 1908

Dear Sir:

You may recall that my wife and I adopted two children from your home five years ago. My wife has been longing for a son or a daughter to replace the boy we lost last year. We read your announcement of the family of four children available for placement. Our daughter has begged us to contact you about taking them into our home. I would prefer to have only the two youngest, but Frances insists that we must take them all. We decided that if we aren't too late in speaking for them, we would be obliged if you would send them to us on the Orphan Train.

We await your decision in this matter.

Your servant,
C. S. Rush

"There is no reason to worry about this home," Mr. Lehman said happily. "I understand that Mr. Rush is a good churchman, and his land is prospering. This is surely an answer to prayer!"

Bert and Ethan didn't doubt that for an instant. With great excitement they made preparations to leave Briarlane. Each of the twelve children was allowed one small bag for his belongings. One set of clothes, in addition to what the child wore, was included.

"You'll stay in Chicago for a few days until the train is ready to finish the trip west," Mr. Lehman told the children. "The good people at Hull-House have made arrangements for you."

On the day of departure, the little group waited to board the train for the first part of their trip. All of them were a bit frightened, but Riley, the acknowledged leader, spoke bravely.

"You all know how to act," he said. "I don't want anyone to disgrace Matron, or he'll answer to me."

Final good-byes were said, and the chosen twelve climbed the steps to the big railcar. Looking out the window, Ethan saw a proud and smiling Hugh standing between his new parents, Patterson and Eugenia Quincy. In his first good suit, Hugh looked handsome indeed.

The train began to move, and Ethan waved to the dear friends he had made over the past year. He looked at Will sitting contentedly beside him, and Simon and Alice on the seat facing him, and thought about all that had happened since the trolley ride that brought them to the Briars in the rain.

What adventures would this new life bring?

Ethan didn't know, but he knew that the Good Shepherd would be with them, and he was content.

When a rockin' concert comes to an end,
the audience might cheer for an encore.
When a tasty meal comes to an end,
it's always nice to savor a bit of dessert.
When a great story comes to an end,
we think you may want to linger.
And so we offer …

… just a little something more after
you have finished a David C Cook novel.
We invite you to stay awhile in the story.
Thanks for reading!

Turn the page for …
- Author's Note
- Write, Talk, Imagine
- About the Author
- Other Books by Arleta Richardson

AUTHOR'S NOTE

In about 1850 New York, New Jersey, Pennsylvania, and other states on the East Coast were troubled by the number of uncared for and abandoned children in their large cities. Orphanages, county poor farms, and foundling homes were filled to capacity. To the annoyance of some and the distress of others, many homeless children lived on the streets, stealing to feed and clothe themselves and running into trouble with the law. Counties were unable to provide for children when the parents had died or couldn't care for them.

In New York, Charles Loring Brace, founder of the Children's Aid Society, began a new system of welfare for orphans and dependent children. His idea was a simple one: Send these abandoned children from the big cities to the western states, which were less populated than the cities, and distribute them to rural families who agreed to take them into their homes.

The children were gathered into groups and placed in railway cars for the trip west. These cars, called Orphan Trains, were life-changing instruments for the thousands of children who rode on them from approximately 1854 to 1929, when the system was abolished. The children were put on display in small towns and villages along the route. Having been notified in advance that the children were coming, families could look them over and choose the ones they wished to take. Children who weren't chosen at one stop continued to the next train stop.

Among those who benefited—or suffered—under those arrangements were four children from a family in Pennsylvania. Ethan, Alice, Simon, and Will Cooper weren't their real names, but the children did indeed live, and Briarlane Christian Children's Home was there to care for them.

In 1992, the real Ethan was ninety-four years of age and remembered some of the details of his early life with clarity. I tried to weave his memories into the story and show how four lives were formed, in part at least, by the circumstances of the days in which they lived.

My thanks and appreciation to Ethan's children for the information they so graciously shared with me. All of them are a wonderful monument to the man Ethan grew up to be.

WRITE, TALK, IMAGINE

Write about It

The Orphan Train offered children a chance for a fresh start. But they would need all their courage to face an unknown future. In what new situation have you had to find courage?

Do you know somebody like Hugh, who tries to control others by threatening them? How do you handle bullies? By understanding Hugh's story and what he really longs for, how might you deal differently with bullies from now on?

At first Ethan doesn't know what to think about God being the Good Shepherd, who has His eye on everyone. Does that idea make you nervous or happy? Why? If you believe God really loves and cares about you, how might that change how you handle hard times?

Talk about It

Ethan was constantly responsible for watching over his younger brothers and sister. When have you been responsible for someone—a sibling, a pet, or a classmate? How did that feel?

Matron says two of the most important things you can say are "thank you" and "I'm sorry." Do you agree? Why or why not? Do you think Hugh should have said "I'm sorry" to Ethan instead of just calling him "a pretty good kid" to make up for being mean to him? Explain.

Bert believes, "It's always best to tell the truth. That way you don't have to keep making up stuff to go with it." Do you think that's true? Why or why not?

Imagine It

Imagine you are going on a journey, and you can only take one small bag of belongings with you, like the children in this story did. What would you choose to take, and why?

Imagine you are Ethan. Hugh asks you to steal the box out of Mr. Lehman's desk drawer. What would you do?

Imagine you are Hugh. Would you apologize to Ethan for being mean to him? Why or why not? And, if so, what would you say?

ABOUT THE AUTHOR

Arleta Richardson grew up on the shores of Lake Michigan, loving the stories her grandmother told about her childhood on a nineteenth-century farm. In the popular Grandma's Attic series, Arleta retold those memories, capturing the hearts and imaginations of more than two million readers around the world.

Fascinated by the history of the Orphan Trains, Arleta based her Orphans' Journey series on the true account of a boy, named Ethan Cooper in the story, who rode the Orphan Train to a new life in 1908. The Orphan Trains operated between 1854 and 1929, relocating about 250,000 orphaned, abandoned, or homeless children.

The themes of Arleta's books reveal what was most important to her—family and friends, doing the right thing, overcoming fear during hard times, and working hard to see dreams fulfilled. She believed that God has a plan for each of us, and that His love and care will be revealed in His perfect timing.

OTHER BOOKS BY ARLETA RICHARDSON

The Grandma's Attic Series

In Grandma's Attic
More Stories from Grandma's Attic
Still More Stories from Grandma's Attic
Treasures from Grandma

Grandma's Attic Novels

Away from Home
A School of Her Own
Wedding Bells Ahead
At Home in North Branch
New Faces, New Friends

Take a Journey Aboard the Orphan Train with the Cooper Children

In the tender style of *Little House on the Prairie*, the Beyond the Orphan Train series tells the story of the Cooper children as they take the orphan train to a new life in the early 1900s. Based on the life of a real family, this charming four-book series is rich in history, adventure, and faith.